Redemption Falls

Ron Day

Ron Day

Published by: Randy House Publishing

ISBN 979-8-9997968-0-6

PUBLISHER'S NOTE

The book is a work of fiction. Names, characters, places, and incidents either are the product of the author's imagination or are used fictitiously, and any resemblance to actual persons, living or dead, business establishments, events, or locales is entirely coincidental.

To Andy…

My Wife

My Support

My Best Friend

and My Lifelong Love

…Thank you.

Prologue

Mornings in Redemption Falls stirred slowly, as if even the sun respected the town's unhurried rhythm. Mist clung to the hollers like a memory refusing to fade, and the air carried the scent of damp earth and woodsmoke. Life here wasn't rushed, it stretched long and lean like the shadows cast by the ridgeline.

Redemption Falls wasn't marked on most maps, and that suited it fine.

The road in curled like a snake, hemmed by mountain laurel and brush-choked ditches... the kind that swallowed headlights whole after dusk. The trees leaned in close this time of year, bare-limbed and bone-colored, their bark flaking like old skin. Wind moved through them in sighs, never full screams, as though the hills didn't believe in drama... only witness.

Some still whispered about the old rites. Said they'd been practiced long before churches outnumbered family names, when blood and ash and breath were part of keeping things still. Most had let them go, folded away like brittle pages in a forgotten book. But a few remembered. Or pretended not to.

Donna Miller had always hated October here. It was the month the light turned brittle. The month the earth stopped pretending it would forgive. She stood at the edge of the porch that morning, coffee in hand, watching mist gather in the hollers like it was plotting something.

Her daddy used to say the fog here was different. That it remembered.

She didn't believe him then. She believed him now.

Chapter 1

Seeking Comfort

The commotion in the small office was violent. A desk drawer slamming shut, shattering the stillness of the house. Papers scattered. Pens clattered to the floor. Something toppled with a thud. Each movement was jagged, frantic, fueled by a rising panic that felt more like desperation than anger.

Donna Miller's hand continued rifling through the bottom drawer of the cherry-wood desk, shoving aside yellowing invoices and dog-eared notepads. Paper scraped like dry leaves beneath her fingers. Somewhere beneath the mess was the pack of Marlboros she'd hidden from Dan last spring. She'd quit for him...a month ago standing in the doorway, watching his hopeful eyes track her every move. But this morning felt different. Missed calls. A spilled coffee, the difficult conversation with her ex-husband, Sam had left her voice shaking. Breathing exercises and mindfulness techniques weren't going to cut it this time. She needed comfort...the old kind.

Her fingertips finally brush crinkled foil. She pulled the pack free, flicked it open, and slipped a cigarette between her lips. It felt unnatural now, but also so familiar, like slipping into an old coat you thought you'd thrown out years ago. Her thumb hovered over the flint of her lighter. It had migrated to the bottom of the drawer too, hidden beneath a church flyer from the previous year. When she touched it, the metal was warm.

She froze...

She hadn't used it. Not since she quit smoking. It should have been cold.

Her brow furrowed, but she shook the thought off and flicked the wheel.

The flame snapped alive with a metallic rasp. It glowed, soft and orange, casting a tremble of shadows onto the nearby wall...a flickering suggestion of movement.

She drew in a deep breath...so deep it was as if her entire body was pulling in the smoke... as if it was her first breath of air after being trapped under water. The smoke invaded her lungs. Relief follows like a tide. Dan wouldn't be home for hours. By then, the haze would be gone. The lie could wait.

The edge came off her breath. Her shoulders unknotted. Her eyes fluttered shut for a second, long enough to forget she was even holding the cigarette. When she opened them again, the smoke curled lazily upward, catching the light. She followed it, tracing its ghostly rise toward the ceiling fan above...off now, but swaying...gently...as if from a draft.

But there was no draft.

Her eyes flicked to the window. Still shut. The air was still.

Donna stared at the fan for a long moment. Her pulse ticked once...hard...behind her ear.

"Just nerves," she said under her breath.

But the nicotine calm couldn't stop her mind from looping back to Sam. Her ex-husband's curt words and menacing tone on the phone after Josh and Michael asked to live with her replayed in her head like a scratched record. Why won't he see they need me? she wonders, drawing another long drag that steadied her shaking hands. Sam had bulldozed through her plea, dismissing her over the crackle of a bad connection. Even so, the boys' voices echoed in her heart: "Mom, please." She owed them this fight.

When the cigarette's ember dimmed, she walked down the hall, the smoke trailing behind her. In the bathroom, the walls painted velvet black; under the harsh vanity light she leaned forward and crushed the butt against porcelain at the sink's edge. She flicked its stub into the toilet and pressed the chrome handle. The swirl of water hypnotized her for a moment before she turned back to the mirror...leaning forward into her reflection bracing her hands on porcelain edge...making eye contact with herself.

There she was: almond-shaped eyes rimmed with fatigue, hair...dark brown and left long and wavy, not having been tended to this morning. Her cheekbones...a little more hollow than last month. No makeup. No mask. Just the raw stuff of living.

But her reflection didn't quite settle.

She blinked.

The woman in the mirror blinked too...but just a beat behind. Not enough to scream about. Just enough to doubt.

Donna tilted her head. The reflection followed, but slower. Like it had to think about it.

Her breath caught.

She leaned closer.

So did the lady in the mirror.

Her pulse skittered. She waited, daring herself to look away, and then look back quickly...the kind of test a child might try in a dark hallway to make sure shadows hadn't moved.

Still there.

Still her.

But her eyes looked...wrong. Brighter maybe. The brown too dark. Something off in the whites. Veined where they shouldn't be.

"You're just tired," she mutters.

Back in the hallway, she waved her arms like a conductor trying to clear the remaining curls of smoke. In the kitchen, off-white appliances with glossy finish. On the countertop lay a crisp business card: Scott Bookout Family Law. She picked it up between thumb and fore-finger, reading and rereading the bold type. Her pulse quickened. With her left hand she cradled the card, and with her right she dialed.

The phone rang twice.

"Bookout Family Law," answered a warm female voice.

Donna swallowed hard. "I need to talk to Mr. Bookout," she said, trying to steady her voice.

Within moments she's scheduled a three o'clock appointment and hangs up, her heart still rattling.

She glanced at the clock on the wall, one thirty, she thought, and strolled into her living room. The white sofa's cushions beckon, and before she knew it, she's lying back, eyelids heavy. Images of her sons warming to her words and of Sam's stubborn silence floated through her drifting mind. The clock ticked away...her breathing slowed, and sleep claimed her.

Donna didn't remember closing her eyes.

She only remembered the warmth of the couch beneath her, the scratch of wool from the throw blanket someone...probably Dan... had left crumpled at the far end. Her legs stretched out on their own. Her breathing slowed.

And then...

She was in the woods...

Not standing...floating. Weightless, drifting just above the ground. Trees crowded around her like ribs, their branches clawing the sky, their trunks leaning inward as if they wanted to whisper. The earth below was soft and black, wet with memory.

Far ahead, she saw a figure.

Indiscernible at first...

Then... as an image in a camera lens coming into focus... Two boys.

One held a flashlight that flickered. The other carried something that looked like a candle, burning low. Their backs were to her. They were walking toward something.

She tried to call out.

No sound came.

The air smelled of pine sap and woodsmoke, but also something sour. Metallic. Old blood or rusted iron.

She floated closer.

The boys stepped into a clearing where a church rose out of the soil like a broken tooth. It leaned slightly to the left, and its windows were black. There was no door. Just darkness yawning inward.

The boys turned to look at her.

Their faces were wrong.

Too smooth. No eyes. Just the idea of faces.

And behind them, in the tower…the bell began to move.

It swung soundlessly. No rope. No wind.

And with each silent arc, the woods grew darker. The trees pulled back. The candle in the boy's hand went out.

Then...

A noise.

Far away.

Closer.

"Hey, wake up sleepy head." Dan leaned in while massaging her shoulder.

All at once Donna gasped and shuttered awake, feeling yanked from her dream without warning... her brown eyes snapped open, framed by thick lashes. She meets his calm blue gazing eyes now bright with surprise, the same shade she once found soothing. Regaining her composure, a soft grin parts her lips, a flash of front teeth. For a heartbeat, contentment fills her chest.

Then… she sits bolt upright. "What time is it?!" she blurts, voice tight with urgency.

Dan blinks at her, tousling his hair. "Um...two-thirty, I think. Why?"

"I have an appointment at three!"

She leaps to her feet, yanks her black coat from the back of a chair, and slings her worn canvas tote over her shoulder. She reaches for Dan's face with both hands, pulls him close, and presses a quick kiss to his lips.

"I love you. I'll explain when I get back."

Dan nods, still blinking, and murmurs, "Okay."

She's already at the door, hand on the knob. As it clicks shut, Dan stands alone in the living room. He inhales twice, frowns, and mutters to himself, "Is some-thing burning?"

Chapter 2

Memories & Family Law

The tires hummed against the pavement as Donna steered onto the winding road toward Bookout Family Law, the dashboard clock ticking too loud in the silence. Outside, the same dogwood trees flanked the shoulder...older now, maybe, or maybe just tired like everything else.

Her fingers tapped the wheel allowing her mind to drift. Then, a song emerged through the static of the radio. The melody curled through the car like a ghost.

She blinked.

And just like that, she was there...a time when things were happier...

...The moon was sharp as a fingernail clipping above Redemption Falls, caught in a web of black-limbed trees. Donna Miller stood in the doorway of the house, coat unzipped, hair pulled into a hasty braid, boots muddy with Tennessee clay. She held her breath and listened. Stillness. Then...

"Mom."

Josh's whisper came from the shadows beside the couch. "Is it time?"

Donna smirked and nodded.

Michael popped up behind him, already wearing his too-big jacket and carrying the flashlight like a sword.

"Don't wake Missy," Donna warned, nodding toward the snoring beagle curled under the table.

Josh opened the door with the reverence of a thief. The three of them slipped out into the night like a secret.

The woods behind the house had no trail, just worn-down roots and wild thistle. Donna knew it by feel...her mother had led her through it years ago, and now it was her turn. Josh led with the flashlight, swinging it side to side like a lightsaber. Michael clung to Donna's sleeve.

"You sure it's okay to go to the old church at night?" Michael asked. "Ain't it haunted?"

"All churches are haunted," Donna said, grinning.

"That's why people go there. So they can talk to the dead relatives."

"Mom," Josh said, rolling his eyes but smiling. "You always gotta make things creepy?"

"Boys who sass their mother get thrown in the baptistry."

They reached the clearing ten minutes later, breath misting. The old white church hunched like a tired ghost, siding peeling, windows boarded. Only the bell tower rose proud, a finger pointing to heaven. The stairs creaked as they climbed, and the bell rope still hung from the ceiling, thick with dust and time.

Michael looked up at it with awe. "It's real."

"Told you," Donna said. "Every woman in our family has rung this bell before her life changed."

Josh grabbed the rope. "Did you do it?"

Donna hesitated, then nodded. "Night before I found out I was pregnant with you."

Michael's eyes widened. "So, what happens if *we* ring it?"

Donna crouched between them. "Nothing. Or maybe everything. Some say it drives the 'lonely ones' back into the woods. Some say it calls them closer. Either way, we light a candle to stay safe."

Josh's grin was all mischief. "Let's do it."

He and Michael pulled the rope together. The bell gave a rusty moan, then a thunderous GONG that echoed down the valley. Birds startled from trees. A dog barked in the distance. Donna laughed...a wild, honest sound she hadn't let out in weeks.

"Now the candle," she said, pulling a red stub from her coat pocket. She struck a match, shielding it from the wind, and lit the wick. The flame flickered weakly, then held.

Josh stared at it. "What if someone sees us?"

Donna wrapped her arm around both boys.

"Then they'll know this family still remembers what matters."

The wind picked up. The candle danced. Donna whispered an old blessing her grandmother taught her...something about dirt and blood and names not being forgotten. She didn't explain it, and the boys didn't ask.

For a few long moments, they stood in silence, watching the flame and listening to the distant echo of the bell fade into the hills.

On the way home, Michael walked in front, braver now, flashlight in hand. Josh lagged behind with Donna.

"You think we'll do this again next year?" he asked.

"I hope so," Donna said.

"You'll always be here, right?"

She didn't answer right away.

"Right?"

Donna smiled tightly and put her arm around him. "Always, baby. Long as the bell still rings."

They didn't hear the sound behind them...a creak of branches that didn't come from wind...or notice the flicker of something watching from the trees. ------------

The only parking space available was the furthest from the law office door, Donna glanced at her watch, 3:02 p.m., then flung open the car door and sprinted across the narrow parking lot. The late-afternoon sun glared off the asphalt, and beads of sweat traced lines down her spine. She passed under a green-and-gold sign bearing tarnished brass letters: Bookout Family Law. Pushing through the glass door, she nearly tripped over the threshold. Inside, the air smelled faintly of lemon cleaner and stale coffee. Heart pounding, she pressed a palm to her jeans and leaned against the wall.

At a small reception desk sat a petite brunette, her dark hair pulled into a neat ponytail. She wore a powder–blue cardigan over a floral blouse and lifted her head from behind a row of manila folders. "May I help you?" she asked, her voice calm.

Donna's breath came in short gasps. "Yes...I have an appointment with Mr. Bookout. I'm Donna Miller."

The receptionist, Sylvia, as a small nameplate read, tapped at her keyboard and ducked behind the half-wall. Moments later, she reemerged with a polite nod. "He's on a call but will be right with you. Please, have a seat." She gestured to a cluster of chairs by the window.

"Water? Coffee?"

Donna's throat felt like sandpaper, but she was too nervous to accept.

"No, thank you," she managed.

She slid into a vinyl chair in the corner. The slick upholstery almost betrayed her, she gripped the arms until her knuckles blanched. Across the room, dusty sunlight filtered through closed blinds, casting striped shadows on faded floral wallpaper. An end table sagged under a stack of dog-eared magazines. She picked up one, let its glossy pages flutter, and stared at a model's vacant smile until the words dissolved.

Footsteps tapped on the hardwood floor. Start-led, she glanced up but saw no one. Then a deep voice beside her said, "Mrs. Miller?"

She jerked upright and slid completely off the chair, landing on her elbows and knees before a broad–shouldered man in a charcoal suit. He had salt–and–pepper hair at his temples, wire–rimmed glasses, and a square jaw softened by concern. "Oh my gosh," she whispered.

"Are you all right?" His Tennessee drawl trembled with genuine worry. He knelt beside her and offered a large hand. "Here let me help you up."

Her cheeks flamed as she accepted his hand. He steadied her, guiding her back into the seat. "That chair's got a mind of its own," he said with a light laugh, tapping the vinyl. "I'll have Sylvia replace it."

"I'm so sorry," she murmured.

"No harm done," he replied. "I'm Scott Bookout. Follow me, please."

He led her down a narrow hallway lined with framed diplomas and yellowing newspaper clippings, headlines like "Fair Advocate for Families." The walls smelled of polished wood and fresh paint. At the end, he opened a heavy mahogany door into his office.

The room felt larger, as if respect and hope were tangible. A tall leather chair sat behind a desk carefully arranged with a sleek laptop, a crystal paperweight, and a neat stack of client files bound by a leather strap. Opposite, two burgundy upholstered chairs waited. Behind him, framed photos: a woman with kind eyes and three children in matching holiday sweaters.

"Please, have a seat," Scott said, settling back. He steepled his fingers atop his stomach and studied her with dark, thoughtful eyes. "Tell me what brings you in today, Mrs. Miller."

Donna settled herself in the chair, drew a breath, and looked at the ornate carpet. "My ex–husband has custody of our sons. I spoke to them this morning they said they want to live with me." Her voice wavered; she pressed fingertips to her lips. "I just want them to be happy."

Scott nodded, tapping a pen on his notebook. "It won't be easy. I need to review the original custody agreement, court transcripts, any documentation you have. Then we'll see if we can petition for a modification."

She leaned forward, a rare flash of determination lighting her eyes. "I know it won't be easy, but it will be worth it."

A gentle smile creased his brow. "Good. To move forward, I'll need a retainer. Sylvia will prepare the paperwork. If you can take care of that today, I'll have everything ready for you to sign in a day or two."

Relief washed over her, easing the tension from her shoulders. "Thank you, Mr. Bookout."

He returned her smile. "Please, call me Scott. Mr. Bookout is my dad."

Donna rose, smoothed her blouse, and followed him back to Sylvia's desk. She handed over her credit card, heard the gentle beep of the swiping machine, then accepted a receipt and a reassuring nod from the receptionist.

Moments later, she slid into her car. The sky beyond the windshield glowed with the soft pink of early evening. She rested her head on the headrest, eyes closed, and let out a long, shaky breath. Fingertips tracing the steering wheel, she whispered to the empty cabin, "Do you know what you're doing?" Her gaze drifted to the ceiling, and for a heartbeat she stayed still. Then she straightened, turned the key, and the engine rumbled to life. With one last steadying breath, she backed out of the parking space and headed home.

The drive home dragged on under a sky smeared with streaks of crimson and slate. Every red light felt endless, each mile marker slipping past like a taunting countdown. When Donna finally eased her car into the familiar gravel of the driveway, her shoulders sagged, and her eyelids fluttered with exhaustion. She practically fell out of the driver's seat pushing the door open and hoisted her scuffed purse off the passenger side, its straps worn thin from years of daily battles.

Inside, the living room was bathed in the pale glow of the television. Dan sat slumped on the sofa in gray sweats, one foot tucked beneath him, the remote hanging limply in his hand. At the sound of her footsteps, he hit "off," and the room went quiet except for the soft tick of the wall clock. His eyes cool blue flecks of concern lifted to meet hers. "So," he said, voice low, "what's goin' on?"

They moved to the round wooden table in the kitchen, its surface nicked and marked by years of coffee rings and hurried scribbles. Donna drew in a shaky breath and laid out the whole story: how she had received a call from the boys, voices full of hope and uncertainty, asking if they could live with her again; the awkward call she'd placed to their father; the tight knot in her chest when she'd finally hung up.

At first, Dan's hands clenched into fists, his jaw tensing as he started to argue, his protective instincts flaring. He opened his mouth ready to point fingers, to map out a solution, but Donna held up a hand. "I don't need you to fix this," she said, her voice steadier than she felt. "I just...need you to listen."

Dan's shoulders dropped. He leaned forward, resting his forearms on the edge of the table. The light of the overhead bulb glinted on his face as he nodded, and for once, he said nothing more. He simply let her speak, occasionally offering a soft, "Mm-hmm," or brushing a fingertip against her hand. The candle… flickering between them cast dancing shadows across the tabletop, and by the time their conversation wound down, only the hush of midnight hovered between them. Their eyes grew heavy, and they drifted off to bed with the echo of unsaid fears still lingering.

------------Dan Miller wasn't from Redemption Falls, he grew up in the Blue Ridge Mountains, the son of a high school science teacher and a park ranger. He inherited a deep respect for the land and a fascination with the unseen forces shaping it. After earning his degrees, Dan spent the first decade of his career working in environmental remediation, helping to clean up old industrial sites and restore polluted waterways in Appalachia.

But after Hurricane Harvey hit in 2017, everything changed.

Dan volunteered on a federal response team to assess environmental damage in the wake of natural disasters. The devastation he saw there changed him fueled a passion not just for recovery, but for prevention. Since then, he's worked as a senior consultant for a global environmental firm, Hathaway-Greene, where his specialty is evaluating environmental risks at disaster sites: landslides, floods, toxic spills. His reports help determine if areas are safe to rebuild or must be permanently abandoned.

His job requires frequent travel...often on short notice. He's flown into hurricane zones, earthquake epicenters, wildfire aftermaths, and coal ash spill sites. The work is difficult...the sites are sometimes unbearable. But it also gives him purpose. He believes that his work helps protect lives...quietly, methodically, behind the scenes.

Dan met Donna a little over a year ago when he came to speak at a regional conference on the environmental fallout of strip mining. Donna, working then as a writer for the local newspaper, had just written a couple of stories on the Hollowing Ground and found Dan to be very interesting.

They married just a few months later. Donna found in Dan someone steady, honest, and unflinchingly decent.

Dan found in Donna a sweet and humble soul, who had the ability to make him laugh.

But the travel gets tiresome and takes its tole on a young marriage. Donna has had to carry the emotional weight of home: longing for more time with her boys, her past and continuing conflict with Sam, the burden of being alone so much and struggling to keep it together. Dan knows it, and it tears at him. He never wanted to be a ghost in his own marriage. He tries to make up for his absences by being present...fully present...when he's home. Quiet dinners, long walks, fixing broken cabinet doors or rickety porch steps. It's not always enough.

Still, Dan is the kind of man who shows up when it counts. Even if he's flying halfway across the country to do it. ----- ---------

Chapter 3

Awakening

Hours later, Donna woke to the frantic buzz of her phone vibrating against the nightstand. She squinted at the digits glowing in the corner of the screen: 4:04 AM. Her thumb hesitated over the answer button as her pulse kicked up. The caller ID read "Shit Head" her private joke for Sam Hayes, each letter mirroring his real initials. For a moment she felt a flicker of dark amusement. Then she pressed "Accept."

Sam's voice slithered through the speaker before she could even say hello. He chuckled, a slow, smug sound and launched straight into his real reason for calling.

"I hear you've hired yourself an attorney," he drawled, words sharp as blades.

He spoke of "dissociative episodes," "manic depression," rattling the diagnoses like ammunition.

"Keep poking around in my world," he warned, "and I'll drag every bit of your therapy into the light. Public record. Front page. Think about how that might...haunt you...and you may discover that there are even worse things than the hell you think you've been living in up until now." Sam's warning echoed like a distant clap of thunder, triggering a smothering emotional weight as she remembered...

-------------The courthouse smelled like old wood and nervous sweat...a mingling of lemon cleaner, mildew, and something colder Donna couldn't name. Something legal and final.

She sat on the left side of the courtroom, hands folded in her lap like her therapist taught her, back straight, shoulders relaxed, expression soft but unreadable. Palms down, fingers still. Don't let them see how badly you're shaking.

Across from her, Sam sat with his attorney, a woman in a tailored gray suit who hadn't smiled once that morning. Sam had smiled, though. Twice. Once at the bailiff, and again when the judge entered. Not smug, just polite. Controlled. Like he was playing the part of the wronged man.

Like he wasn't the one who broke things in the first place.

Donna's lawyer...public defender, overworked and stretched too thin...leaned close, whispering, "Stay calm. Speak only when asked. They're going to hit your therapy hard, but you've got documentation."

She nodded; lips pressed tight. But her eyes drifted to the empty bench behind her. No one had come. Her one friend, Jess couldn't make it. Dan hadn't known her then. No other friends. Not anymore. Sam had seen to that over the years...slow erosion, one accusation at a time.

The judge, a middle-aged man with a tired mustache and kinder eyes than she'd expected, shuffled through the paperwork. "We're here today to consider primary custody of Joshua and Michael Hayes, ages five and six. Petition brought forward by the father, Mr. Samuel Hayes."

Sam's attorney stood. "Your Honor, we submit into record the psychological evaluations and treatment history of the respondent, Mrs. Donna Hayes. Over a six-month period, she was under the care of Dr. Thomas Griffith for what was diagnosed as depression with dissociative tendencies, including two noted memory blackouts and a documented prescription overdose."

Donna's breath caught. The room seemed to constrict. Blackouts. That word was always heavier when spoken by strangers.

The attorney continued, voice crisp and professional. "Furthermore, Dr. Griffith's notes" she held up a manila folder like a scalpel "indicate recurring delusions, described as 'a sense of being watched,' and 'auditory disturbances' that the patient attributed to inherited sensitivity. Your Honor, we assert this pattern reflects a potential risk to the well-being of the minor children."

Donna blinked rapidly, gripping the arms of her chair. She wanted to speak, wanted to scream those notes weren't meant for this...but her throat locked.

The judge turned to her. "Mrs. Hayes, would you like to respond?"

She rose slowly. Her knees buckled for half a second, then locked into place. The silence felt thick and sour. She looked toward Sam...he met her eyes without flinching, that familiar smirk buried behind the performance of conccrn.

"I sought help," she said, voice steady despite the tremble in her hands.

"After years of emotional neglect. After being gaslit. I did the hard work. I got better. My therapist said I'd made progress. But none of that is in the folder they just showed you."

The judge didn't interrupt. He just watched.

Donna continued. "The overdose was an accident. Two medications in similar bottles. My pharmacist admitted it. But it was filed under 'incident,' and now it's being weaponized."

She looked down. Then back up, eyes fierce now.

"Sam Hayes treats his sons like property, like tokens to be used in some twisted game."

Sam's attorney stood, objecting.

"Speculation, Your Honor."

The judge held up a hand. "Let her finish."

Donna swallowed hard. "All I want is to be allowed to be their mother…to care for them."

The courtroom went quiet. Old…nefarious, un-seen shadows seemed to take center stage… as Sam stood, slow and measured, adjusting the cuffs of his white shirt. He stepped forward, hands folded in front of him. The air around him felt unnaturally still. Not heavy, not loud…just… suspended. Like the courtroom itself held its breath.

Donna caught it, a prickle behind her eyes, a sense of pressure on her temples as if the walls had leaned in closer to listen.

"Your Honor," Sam began, voice smooth as river-stone, "this isn't about punishing Donna."

As he spoke, the fluorescent light above flick-ered...not enough to draw attention, but enough to make Donna's vision stutter. In that sliver of darkness, she saw something behind Sam. A shadow out of place, like someone standing just over his shoulder, tall, motionless and long-limbed. When the lights returned, it was gone.

"I love my boys," Sam continued, tone measured. "But I can't in good conscience send them into a home where their mother can't tell what's real and what's not."

Donna blinked hard, the edges of her vision blurring as if the air itself had shifted. For a heartbeat, something unnatural flashed across her mind...a jagged, foreign image, like a shard of memory not her own, slicing through her thoughts with the ferocity of lightening clawing across a storm-dark sky. It left a metallic taste on her tongue and the faint scent of scorched earth in its wake.

Sam's eyes had found hers, and for a second too long, they held.

Not angry. Not smug.

Just... certain.

A certainty born of something colder than confidence.

_____

Donna's conscious mind returned to the present and the call... Sam's voice still lingered like a stench in the air. Donna felt her chest tighten, a heavy weight settling at the pit of her stomach. After a long, deliberate pause, she whispered,

"Yes, I suppose so..." Her voice cracked on the last word.

She tapped the red button, cut the line, and let the phone fall back onto the mattress. Lying on her side, she stared at the pale circle of light on the wall, feeling the old dread coil itself around her heart.

She'd clawed her way back from that dark place, through coping skills, support groups, midnight journal entries and finally believed she was free.

But Sam's call had cracked open the past, and now the darkness threatened to seep in once more. _____

She moved with the kind of intention that silenced questions before they fully formed as she rose from her bed. Behind her, Dan's voice barely registered "Who was that? Where are you going?" but she didn't answer. A flick of her wrist, a faint wave of her hand over her shoulder, was all he got. Not now.

The floor, cool and polished beneath her feet, reflected just enough light to shimmer beneath the glide of her step. Her nightgown whispered against her legs, the satin catching slivers of moonlight like ripples on a midnight stream. The hallway stretched ahead, quiet and narrow, swallowing the soft patter of her movement.

Inside the office, she closed the door behind her with a click too soft for the weight she carried. Her breath caught in her throat. The first tear slid down before she reached the window, trailing a path through the silence.

She stood still before the glass, hands curled loosely at her sides, gaze locked on the yard beyond. The trimmed grass lay still in the glow of the streetlamps, but it was the wire overhead that held her attention, two crows perched in rigid symmetry, eyes glinting like beads of coal. They didn't move. Didn't blink. Just watched.

So did she.

She counted the feathers on their wings, followed the rise and fall of their sleek black chests. Something in their stillness spoke to her, quiet and ancient. So many seconds clicked by as Donna seemed to be drawn deeper into this gaze.

And then they were gone, lifting in perfect unison, wings slicing the air as they vanished into the night sky. She followed their path until they dissolved into the dark. Upward. Away. Untethered.

Her reflection in the window blurred as tears welled again. She didn't wipe them. Her arms down at her sides…fists clenched and trembling now. Her breath shortened, shallow. The heat in her cheeks climbed fast, flushing her skin, jaw tightening until the pressure made her teeth ache. Her shoulders shook. Her eyes squeezed shut against it all, and the tears poured freely, hot, unrelenting.

Then…stillness.

She froze.

Donna's eyes snapped open; her breathing stopped. Her stare fixed somewhere far past the window, far beyond the crows, past the yard, past the world.

Her lips parted, trembling. And in a breath so soft it barely stirred the air, a name slipped free with a whisper…

Chapter 4

This Life Has Me by the Throat

He stood on the masonry-paved dock, the rough stones pressing into his boot soles. Dawn spilled across the lake in ribbons of rose and amber, turning the water's gentle swell into a slow dance. The motion underfoot and the shimmer on the surface tugged at a childhood memory; canoes cutting through misty mornings, the snap of twigs, the tang of river pine in the air.

A soft whimper yanked him from nostalgia. At his feet, a woman knelt, wrists knotted with coarse rope, a frayed gag stifling her sobs. He lowered himself beside her, his sleeve brushing stone dust. His left hand stroked her cheek, fingertips cold against her skin, wet with tears, while his right hand held the revolver, its silencer still resting heavy and unforgiving in his palm.

"If it were up to me, darlin', I'd let you live." He tipped his head, voice smooth with southern drawl.

"This isn't' really me."

He rose in one fluid motion, the barrel sliding against her temple. A muted pop echoed across the water. Her body went limp and slipped off the dock's edge, the cinder block tied to her ankle dragging her into the lake. Tiny rings of ripples fanned outward, then folded back into glass. He crouched once more, as if to brush a farewell across the spot where her hair had disappeared beneath the waves. Then he stood, coat tails snapping behind him, and strode toward the shore.

Beau Carter caught his own hollow reflection in the black SUV's side mirror, the glass bending his face into something half-recognizable. He'd worn many skins since leaving the military…mercenary, courier, ghost in the margins…but none had clung to him like this one. The killer's skin. It wasn't a title he'd ever claimed aloud, but it hung around his neck all the same, heavy as a noose and twice as tight.

It hadn't started that way. The first job as a contractor had felt clinical, almost abstract…just intel, just a name. A necessary evil for someone with no other way to disappear. But the next came easier. Cleaner. And by the third, he'd stopped asking why.

Regret lived in him now like a second set of lungs…silent most days, but there when the world quieted down. Coiled in his chest, pressing against his ribs every time he lifted the gun. He told himself it was survival. That he was only taking out worse people. But that didn't change the way the muzzle felt in his hand. Heavy. Familiar. Unforgiving.

This life had him by the throat. And sometimes, late at night when the adrenaline faded and silence came creeping, Beau wondered if it always had.

At the Princess Motel, the neon sign flickered orange against peeling vinyl siding. He eased his SUV onto cracked concrete, the engine ticking in the chill. Through the open window drifted the musty scent of mothballs and mildew. He climbed out of the SUV…with a bottle of whiskey in one hand…his nightly companion… and a duffle bag in the other, he pushed through the lobby door.

Sunlight slanted through dusty windows, re-vealing boxes stacked against one wall and a small TV perched on a worn countertop. Beau leaned on the chip-ped Formica and waited. The floorboards moaned.

"Hey there!" came a scratchy voice. A portly man emerged from a back room, shirt rumpled, yellow teeth glinting. "Sorry, mister, didn't hear ya." He wiped a hand on his pants. "Name's Harold."

"Beau Carter," he replied.

Harold pecked at an ancient keyboard, then slid a clipboard forward. "Sign here. How long you stayin'?"

"Just the night," Beau said, scrawling his name. "Then I'm gone."

"Where to?"

"Home," Beau answered, voice flat.

Harold arched an eyebrow. "Far from here, huh." He thrust a flimsy plastic key card at him. "Room twelve. Dial zero if you need anything."

Beau nodded and found room 12 at the end of a flickering hallway. Inside, the carpet was threadbare, wallpaper peeling, a single lamp spilling yellow light across a sagging bed. A small color TV sat on the dresser; picture grainy with static. He dropped his duffel; the zipper rasped. He lowered himself onto the edge of the mattress, boots crunching on a stray pebble.

He stared at the floor. After a long moment, he covered his face with his hands.

A slow, relentless pressure coiled in Beau's chest, as if something with cold, pearled teeth had sunk in and refused to let go. Regret chewed through him with patient cruelty, every bite hollowing him out a little more. He clenched his jaw, but the memory came anyway…uninvited, merciless…rising from the dark like smoke from a battlefield long buried.

_____Kandahar Province, 2010----The sun was a white disc bleeding through the haze, the air thick with heat and rot. Beau crouched behind a half-crumbling wall; his knuckles white on the grip of his M4. The comms in his ear hissed with static. Dust clung to his skin like guilt.

"Two targets. Building left of the minaret," came the whisper from Sarge. "Orders are to clear. No exceptions."

Beau moved on instinct. Room by room. Door by door. They'd done this a dozen times in a dozen villages...sweeps, they called them. Security. Peacekeeping.

The boy couldn't have been more than ten.

Beau hadn't even seen the old radio clutched in his tiny hands until it was too late. A crackled voice came through it, shouting coordinates in a language Beau barely understood. Then movement, too fast, too desperate.

He pulled the trigger.

Three rounds. Center mass. The boy crumpled soundlessly, eyes still wide with surprise, or maybe confusion. A toy truck fell from his pocket and bounced across the floor.

Sarge barked something...secure the building, keep moving, but Beau didn't hear it. He was staring at the blood spreading beneath the child, dark and glistening, soaking into the cracked tiles like it had been waiting for this.

Later, they'd say the boy was a runner. A spotter for the Taliban. That the radio had enemy chatter. That Beau saved lives.

But none of that stuck.

What stuck was the way the mother wailed when she found him. The way her cries didn't sound human, like something had been ripped from her throat and hurled into the sky.

What stuck was how Beau couldn't remember the boy's face now, only his hands...small, dirt-streaked, twitching as the life leaked out of him.

That night, sitting on the desert floor, under a dead sky, Beau smoked until his fingers trembled, trying to feel something other than hollow. Trying to pretend there was still a line between him and the people they were fighting.

Suddenly a recollection of a brother in arms who he had fought along side. Sgt. Ogle...Sgt. Tommy Ogle...was there to get him through this kind of mind sink many times. Until Tommy was killed in that same godforsaken place. Beau had been with Tommy in his last moments after suffering a neck wound...shrapnel from an IED. Suddenly the memory of the promise that he had made to Tommy as he died invaded his consciousness...a promise that had not been kept. _____

Now, here in this tiny, tattered hotel room, sitting on that bed, Beau's shoulders began to shake, then his whole body trembled. He slid down until he lay curled on the bed, arms wrapped tight around his knees. Sobs wracked him, leaving wet patches on the faded bedspread. He remained there through the night, carried off only by waves of despair and the steady hum of the old television.

Chapter 5

Where Is It?

The air in the study was heavy, thick with the scent of old paper, varnish, and something sharper beneath it, like panic sweat and dust stirred from long-forgotten corners. Sam Hayes stood in the center of the room, surrounded by shelves that groaned under the weight of ledgers, journals, and boxes marked in spidery handwriting that hadn't belonged to anyone living in decades.

He yanked open drawer after drawer, flinging them shut with hollow bangs that echoed down the hallway. Pages scattered in his wake, some torn, others yellowed and brittle with age. The room looked ran-sacked, because it was.

His hands trembled as he snatched a leather-bound volume from the shelf, cracked it open, skimmed it, cursed, and tossed it onto a growing pile of discards. Genealogies. Land deeds. Ritual logs. Letters written in script so faded it looked like whispers trapped on the page. All relics of a bloodline that had stretched back to the founding of Redemption Falls, maybe further.

But not what he needed.

"Where is it?!" he snarled, voice ragged, almost hoarse.

The desperation clung to him like the humidity of a storm about to break. He turned and swept the edge of a desk clear with one wild motion, sending an ornate brass candlestick and a stack of handwritten rites crashing to the floor.

He stopped, breath heaving. The silence that followed rang louder than the chaos had.

"She's starting to develop a spine," he hissed through clenched teeth, as if the very idea disgusted him. "That cannot happen. Not now. Not after everything."

He ran both hands through his hair and stared at the room like it had betrayed him. That book, the one passed down through his bloodline, full of bindings, dominions, ancestral protections...it was supposed to be here. Safeguarded. Accounted for.

But it was gone.

And Donna was slipping out from under his thumb.

The floor creaked beneath his boots as he turned slowly, scanning the shelves again, this time more like a man haunted than hurried. His fingers hovered in the air, unsure where to turn next.

For the first time that evening, Sam Hayes looked less like a man in control of a powerful legacy and more like someone watching it fall apart in his hands.

The bell above the door at The Book Nook gave its usual rusted jingle as Ruthie Lynn elbowed it open, her arms full of a cardboard box worn soft at the edges. It had *Storage -Back Study* scribbled on the side in faded marker, the letters nearly rubbed off by time and hands.

"Where should I put this one, Jess?" Ruthie called, nudging the box onto the counter with a huff. "Another haul. Think this is the last of it."

Jess Porter, sorting through a stack of romance paperbacks by the register, barely looked up. "Anywhere back by the donation shelf. I'll sort it tomorrow."

"Alright, but fair warning, some of it's strange. Like, old-strange."

Ruthie wandered toward the end, passing rows of unevenly shelved books and gently flickering string lights. She set the box down on a cart with wheels to be gone through later.

Inside, among the water-stained recipe cards, brittle hymnals, and old receipts stuffed into forgotten envelopes, was a thick, leather-bound volume. Its spine was cracked but intact, the cover embossed with a symbol few would recognize now. The title was, barely legible unless you held it at just the right angle in the light. There were no page numbers, only sigils, faded ink, and margins scribbled with the careful notes of multiple generations.

Ruthie didn't notice any of that. She pulled out a ragged copy of Little Women instead, flipped through it absentmindedly, and left the rest untouched.

As Ruthie turned to walk away...a whisper...she paused. Turning back toward the box of donated items, listened...

There it was a gain...a voice...so faint Ruthie was unable to make out what it was saying.

"Jess?" She called out.

"Yep!" came Jess' voice from the front of the store.

"N... nothing. Just thought you said something." Ruthie explained as she managed a nervous chuckle under her breath.

Ruthies gaze stayed fixed on the box for a few seconds longer.

Again, the whisper came...unintelligible but not imagined.

Ruthie immediately broke her gaze, turned and headed for the front of the store with quick, nervous steps.

"I'll be keeping this little episode to myself." She said under her voice.

She quickly walked past the front counter where Jess was still sorting paperbacks and out the front door as Jess watched...

"Ru..." she couldn't get Ruthie's name out before the bells above the door had chimed with Ruthies exit. Jess looked confused but shrugged it off and continued her sorting.

Meanwhile, the book...settled quietly into its new place among the forgotten and discarded. No wards activated. No warnings sounded. Just the soft tick of the overhead clock and the quiet hum of a floor fan turning side to side.

Outside, the sky was darkening, and back at the Hayes house, Sam Hayes was still tearing through drawers, unaware that centuries of power and control now sat tucked away in a cardboard box, waiting for someone else to pick it up.

Ron Day

Chapter 6

Unbidden Laughter

Dawn filtered through the blinds in pale gold slats, casting stripes across Donna's closed eyelids. She blinked awake, slowly, as though surfacing from a dream too deep to name. Her body ached. She lay curled on the narrow leather sofa in her home office, its cushions stiff and unforgiving beneath her spine. The smell of old ink and sun-warmed vinyl clung to the air. Her cheek, when she lifted her head, peeled softly away from the leather arm of sofa leaving a red mark on her cheek. Tuesday. Or maybe Thursday. The numbers swam.

How long had she been here?

The question rose unbidden, then slipped away before she could catch it. Donna sat up stiffly, bones creaking like old floorboards, and took a breath that trembled in her chest. From the kitchen came the hiss of something frying, the fatty crackle of bacon in a hot skillet, mingled with the sweet tang of cooked eggs. A normal sound. Comforting, even. But her heart raced anyway. Her fingers trembled in her lap.

She squinted toward the light, blinking hard. The last thing she could remember...truly remember...was laying in bed with the phone pressed to her ear, Sam's voice slithering through the line. Low. Venomous. Then... nothing. Not even a blur. Just a clean slice in her memory, like a scene edited from film. The cold on her back. The unfamiliar feeling of the couch under her spine. Her pulse thrummed at her temples like a warning.

She forced herself upright and wandered barefoot into the kitchen, the cool tile shocking against her soles. Dan stood at the stove, sleeves rolled up, a wooden spatula in one hand. His other hand rested on the counter, tapping rhythmically. He turned as she entered, steam curling from his dark hair, and smiled… slow and steady, like everything was fine. Like she hadn't just lost hours.

Her lips twitched into a return smile that didn't quite reach her eyes.

Without a word, Dan plated breakfast…crisp bacon curling like sleeping fingers, golden eggs glistening with butter…and handed her a plate. They moved through the motions like dancers rehearsing an old, familiar choreography. Sit. Fork. Chew. Swallow. Repeat.

At the table, silence settled between them like fog. Only the soft clinks of cutlery, the low hum of the refrigerator, and Dan's calm breathing filled the room. Donna stared at the food, unsure whether she was hungry or just pretending.

When the plates were clean and the silence had stretched too long, Dan cleared his throat. "What's your plan today?" he asked, eyes on the dishes, not her.

Donna blinked. Her mind was a blank slate smeared with half-faded notes. "I... I'm not sure," she murmured, twisting the napkin in her lap until it tore. The house would be hollow without him. Too quiet. Too alive. Something in the walls seemed to breathe when she was alone...always had. But lately it had begun to whisper.

Dan checked his watch and stood. "I've got to head out. Galveston this time...week-long conference." He glanced at her, something like regret in his eyes. "I'll call once I land."

Her chest tightened. She reached across the table, but the movement faltered halfway, and her hand dropped uselessly into her lap. "Could you stay?" Her voice was barely audible, as if speaking it too loudly would make it too real. "I don't want to be alone right now."

Dan's mouth pressed into a thin line. He hesitated, then shook his head softly. "If I had a choice..."

"I know," she said. And she did. Or thought she did.

He kissed her forehead, a light brush of lips that grazed her skin, then walked toward the door looking back.... "I love you, and I'll miss you." he said.

Donna followed him to the garage and stood barefoot on the concrete, watching as his white sedan rolled away. The taillights blinked red at the stop sign, then disappeared into the morning haze. She stood motionless in the open air, sun striking her nightgown, catching specks of dust that shimmered like flecks of gold. She watched them drift and settle. Her breath caught…there, again, that whisper. Too faint to name, too close to ignore.

She turned slowly and walked back into the house.

The television in the living room stood dark. The walls, silent. Or almost. In the office, the cigarette pack lay waiting beside her laptop, half-empty. She took one, lit it, and drew a deep breath. Smoke filled her lungs like fog rolling over a cold moor. She exhaled slowly, staring at the patch of sunlight now creeping across the floor.

But still...nothing. No memory of the hours before waking. No sense of how she'd crossed from one moment to the next. She hadn't fallen asleep. She hadn't meant to sit down. There had been the phone call. Sam. Then silence. Then this.

Donna pinched the bridge of her nose, trying to massage the ache behind her eyes. The world around her felt unfamiliar...edges too sharp, colors slightly off. Like a dream remembered wrong. Like the room itself was waiting for her to remember something buried deep in her blood.

Shopping might help. The thought floated into her mind uninvited. Bright lights, people, motion. She clung to it like a raft. Maybe she just needed a distraction.

But then her mouth moved on its own. The words slipped out, quiet and crystalline, falling like glass beads onto the desk.

"Shopping for a gun."

Her eyes widened. The sentence hung in the air, foreign and intimate. She looked at her reflection in the darkened computer screen. Her pupils were too wide.

Then a sound bubbled up from her throat...a laugh. At first, it was a soft chuckle, dry and brittle. But it built, grew...unraveled. It spilled out of her in waves, raw and breathless, until her body shook with it. Laughter echoed off the walls, too loud in the still house. Her fingers clutched the arms of the chair, her head tilted back as the tears came...unwelcome and hot.

She laughed like something inside her had cracked wide open, and the thing inside was finally free.

And somewhere...deep, dormant, old as bone...some-thing stirred.

Donna eased her sedan down the driveway with a false steadiness in her grip, a vow whispered under her breath to find distraction...maybe a coffee, maybe a blouse in a color she hadn't worn since the divorce. Something light. Something pointless. Something to rinse the taste of yesterday from her mind. But the sky, low and leaden, had its own intentions. The clouds pressed against the horizon like bruises. Every stoplight she passed flared in her windshield like interrogation lamps, as though the town itself had decided to look too closely.

Her pulse fluttered unexpectedly. Flashbulb mem-ories sparked behind her eyes...Sam's voice and tone, the twist of his mouth when he'd accused her of forgetting things, of vanishing from her own life. Laughter, unhinged and unfamiliar, rang in her ears. Her hands tightened on the wheel. She shook her head and exhaled through her teeth, trying to breathe herself back into her body.

At some point, her car drifted onto Oak Street. She didn't remember turning.

The sign came into view before she realized where she was going...Twin Oaks Church. The clean white clapboard walls rose from the ground like they'd been planted there by old hands. The steeple, slender and sharp, stabbed upward into the gray sky like a finger pointing past the clouds. Donna felt her stomach lurch. Her foot came off the accelerator of its own accord as she turned into the lot by the church...she was there to see someone...

_____ On a typical Sunday, the gravel lot beside Twin Oaks Chapel filled before the first bell. Families arrived in rusted pickups, Bibles worn soft by time, nestled beneath arms, and children dressed in stiff collars and patent leather shoes. The congregation didn't just worship together...they breathed the same faith, deep and generational, rooted as firmly as the old oaks behind the church.

But beneath the hymns and handshakes, there were murmurs. Not spoken, exactly, just felt. A prickle at the nape of the neck while walking alone at dusk. A door creaking open on windless nights. Cold spots in warm kitchens. These weren't things people talked about in the light, but everyone knew the stories. A soldier seen weeping in the woods decades after the war. A pale face in the mirror that vanished when you turned. And always, always the whispers of the Sin Eaters, those strange, spiritually endowed figures who once walked the ridges and hollers, taking on the sins of the dying in exchange for peace.

The old ways didn't die when the settlers crossed the sea...they clung like sap to their boots, followed them into the hollers and high ridgelines, settling deep into the cracks of this new land. What they carried wasn't just folklore or prayer, but something older rituals that hummed beneath the skin, rites whispered by firelight in tongues not spoken in daylight. They wove those dark threads into the fabric of Appalachian life, quietly, persistently, until belief and blood became the same thing.

The land here remembers.

It took those rites like roots take to soil...absorbing every echo of them. And something in the earth held on. Not with reverence, but with a slow, festering hunger. The ground beneath Redemption Falls doesn't forget the cost of old magic. It cradles it. Broods over it. Like a wound never allowed to scab.

You can feel it if you're still enough...standing alone in the fog...maybe...or walking past the old stone circles where nothing grows. It's not loud, but it's there. A hum. A weight. A knowing.

Folks here don't talk much about it. Not in church. Not over coffee. But they all know. Some things never left these mountains. They only went quiet...

Pastor Jim Crowder never spoke of them. Not in the pulpit, not in private. Ten years he'd led the flock at Twin Oaks, ever since his father passed the pulpit down like a torch. His sermons were steady, his manner calm, his faith dependable, but somewhere along the way, the fire had dulled... maybe a little too comfortable. He mowed the church grounds on Thursdays and met with the hurting on Wednesdays. He smiled, nodded and prayed.

But when he locked the chapel doors at night, he felt it; that same oppressive stillness that settled over Redemption Falls after dark. _____

She parked without thinking. The engine ticked in protest as it cooled. As she climbed the three front steps, the boards gave a hollow thunk beneath her boots...an echo that reverberated longer than it should have. The scent of damp leaves and oiled wood filled her nose. Her fingers closed over the cool brass lever on the heavy chapel door. The moment before she pushed it open stretched long and strange, as if something on the other side was holding its breath.

The door opened Inward.

"Donna." Pastor Jim's voice emerged from the dim stillness, low and smooth like a river that knew all its bends. He stood under the slope of the rafters, framed in the wavering glow of an oil lantern that hung by the door. The light painted him in tarnished gold, but the warmth didn't reach his eyes. His smile was slow to form...habitual rather than heartfelt. "You startled me."

Donna hovered in the doorway. Her fingers tugged at the edge of her jacket. "I... didn't plan to come," she admitted. "I just... ended up here." The sentence felt too true. Like something had drawn her, not for comfort but for reckoning.

Jim's eyes stayed on her a moment too long. Then he stepped aside. "Come in out of the cold."

He closed the door behind her, and the silence of the sanctuary wrapped around them like velvet. The pews gleamed in symmetrical rows, hymnals tucked neatly in place, every detail precisely as it had been for decades. The stained-glass windows bled bruised purples and blood-wine reds across the floors. Donna's shadow fractured beneath her feet.

Pastor Jim didn't speak as he led her to the small side office...a place used more often for grief than guidance. A kettle hissed on a hot plate, steam curling like incense. He poured the boiling water into mismatched mugs where it mixed with the instant coffee he had waiting. The one he handed her bore a chip in the rim, a spiderweb of cracks beneath the glaze. Donna ran her thumb along it.

They sat in worn chairs, their legs nearly touching, the desk between them cluttered with prayer cards, sermon notes, and a Bible that looked more ceremonial than read. The air smelled faintly of old books and cedar.

Donna talked. Slowly, cautiously. About Sam. About the custody hearing. About the gaps in her memory...the missing hours, the feeling that someone else had briefly taken her place. She confessed the creeping sense of displacement, of watching her own life from a distance she couldn't close. Her voice barely rose above the hum of the kettle, as if saying it too loud might bring a tone of finality.

Pastor Jim listened; mug cradled in both hands like an offering. He nodded in the right places, murmured verses that tasted seemed appropriate for the context. When he spoke of rest, of solitude, of God's plan, his voice thinned into something echoic and empty, like a room meant to feel sacred but long since hollowed out.

And when Donna asked about memory...about losing it, about darkness settling in like fog...his posture shifted... just a little. A tremor in the stillness.

"There are things," he said slowly, not quite meeting her gaze, "better left in God's hands."

But Donna heard the hesitation in his tone. The buried knowing. She saw the flicker in his eyes, the way they darted once toward the corner of the room...as though expecting something to rise from it.

This silence wasn't born of ignorance. It was born of blood debts. Of rites too old to name in daylight. Of ancestral pacts folded into the foundations of this town like dry leaves in cement.

Pastor Jim had been taught to forget. But forgetting was not the same as unknowing.

When she finally stepped back into the cold, Donna wasn't comforted. The questions clung to her like fog on wool. How had Sam known about her lawyer? Why had Jim's hands trembled when he quoted scripture? And why...deep in the marrow of her bones...did she sense he was steeling away old memories of darker things.

Chapter 7

Pastor's Burden

After Donna left the chapel, Pastor Jim stood in the side office for a long while without moving. The kettle on the hot plate had begun to hiss again, water bubbling low and angry. He didn't move to silence it. He just stared at the empty chair across from his desk, the one Donna had occupied minutes earlier.

He could still smell the ghost of her presence…candle wax, paper, old fear rekindled. His fingers tightened around the chipped mug. The glaze fractured beneath his grip.

He whispered, "Lord, don't make me do this again."

But no answer came. Only the echo of his voice bouncing off the paneled walls like the fading tail of a hymn. Pastor Jim moved purposefully to the bookshelf. Behind a row of tattered devotionals and weathered copies of Streams in the Desert, he found what he was looking for...a worn manila folder, its corners curled and stained with age. He hesitated before pulling it out. When he finally laid it on the desk, he stared at the handwritten label:

Crowder, James – 1977 Incident Report

His hand hovered above the flap. Then with a slow exhale, he opened it.

Inside was a photograph...grainy, black and white. A boy no older than seven stood at the edge of a wooded trail, his face caught mid-turn. The image was blurred, like it had been taken too quickly. In the background, something darker loomed in the trees, barely visible. Not quite a shape. Not quite a shadow.

But definitely there. Jim swallowed hard. He knew what it was. They had told him it was just a fever dream. That he'd wandered too far from the church picnic and got turned around. That the thing he saw…tall, dark, long-fingered and voiceless…was a trick of light through old pine. But he remembered the sound it made when it moved. Not footsteps. A hum. A low, bone-deep sound like something ancient vibrating just beneath the skin.

He'd buried that memory under decades of scripture and structure… Sunday sermons, marriage counseling, the occasional funeral. He told himself he was a man of God, not a keeper of ghosts.

But Redemption Falls didn't let go of its old debts. And lately, he'd felt the soil shift under his feet. Jim sat down heavily, flipping to the next page. A report from a church elder. "Boy found near the old stone circle. Disoriented. Nonverbal for three hours. Repeated phrase: 'He was watching.' No visible injuries. Recovered by sunset."

Below it, a note in a different hand. Slanted. Sharper.

"He saw the Hollowed One. He needs to forget. Prayer and time." Jim clenched his jaw.

He hadn't forgotten. Not for one second.

And now Donna had come into the church with eyes wide from knowing too much… not enough. Carrying a weight that smelled of old paper and ink-drawn pacts. He recognized it on her. The same way he'd once seen it on his father in the pulpit, back when fire and brimstone were more than metaphor. Jim rose and crossed to the altar. He knelt, not because he felt holy, but because his legs were shaking.

His fingers brushed the old Bible beneath the pulpit…the one his grandfather used when the congregation still whispered about sin-eaters and how they walked the high ridges. The one with pressed herbs between the pages and names scribbled in the margins.

He flipped It open to the Inside cover. There it was. His grandfather's handwriting faded but legible. "Some sins don't die. They wait." Jim closed his eyes. He whispered a name. Not Donna's. Not his own. But the name he'd heard in a dream three nights ago…spoken by a voice that wasn't his, in a place between waking and something else.

"Asa." And the shadows in the chapel shifted, just slightly, like something had turned its head to listen.

Chapter 8

His Rightful Inheritance

The basement of the old rectory still smelled like copper and mildew.

Sam stood barefoot on the stone floor, sleeves rolled up, salt drying on his skin. The air down here never warmed. It clung to the bones. Made the skin remember things. He touched the edge of the circle he'd chalked in the dust...carefully drawn, lined with broken corn husks and the ash of last Sunday's offering. He'd always favored ash. Something about it whispered of sacrifice. Of aftermath. Above him, the house was silent. His boys were staying the night at a friend's house. It created the space of time he needed. "She doesn't understand what they carry," he muttered. The words echoed off the stone.

He moved to the wooden crate tucked under the old furnace. Inside were remnants he'd kept hidden for years…carefully wrapped in cloth and dark oil: the tooth from that first deer that bled wrong. A bottle of muddy river water. A child's bib, unwashed. And the page.

The torn page from a very old book. He'd burned the rest of the entry years ago, convinced it would lead to questions he didn't want asked. But this page he kept. Not out of sentiment. Out of necessity.

He unfolded it now. The script was nearly illegible in the flickering light. Cursive ink curled and brown, like it had bled.

"To take the burden is to take the power. The bearer shall walk as both witness and warden. But to take it without rite… is theft. And theft leaves a wound that does not close." Sam stared at the word theft. His eyes twitched.

He hadn't stolen anything. He'd taken what no one else had the courage to.

He was sixteen when he first saw the rite. His grandmother...Ruth Hayes...had been the last known practitioner. She'd whispered prayers over dying animals, left blood on the lintel when storms came, and kept a jar of ash behind every window.

He watched her In secret one winter night, out behind the canning shed. A stillborn calf lay on a white sheet, steam rising from its flank. She touched its brow, smeared its tongue with honey, and whispered words that made his skin crawl. When she died, no one came to claim the tools. No one asked how she'd been burying the dreams of a town. So, Sam learned. From the margins. From what was left in journals and whispers. From pain. And when his father drank himself into silence, Sam took the rite for himself.

He didn't do It all at once. That"' what others never understood. The rite wasn't some firework...it was erosion. A wearing-down. An assumption. He tried it on a dying dog first. It whimpered. Then it lay still. And he heard...faint and terrible…the echo of something not quite prayer rise up from the floorboards later that night. That was power. That was the edge of it. And over time, he learned to use it. To bind. To mark.

He walked through Donna's dreams once, early on, when she still laughed too loud and fought him in court with too much fire in her belly. He left the smell of mud on her pillow. Let her believe it was nerves, trauma, stress. She called it grief. He called it inheritance. Now, he stepped into the circle. The dust rose around his ankles like breath. He whispered a name…not hers, not the boys'…but his own. "Samuel Josiah Hayes." The air shifted. From the rafters, something creaked. A presence stirred. He didn't flinch. Instead, he smiled. "I know what I carry," he said softly. "And I know what I'll leave behind."

He reached for the small mirror beside the ash dish. His own face stared back…sharp, hollow-eyed, yet certain. He pressed his thumb into the center of the glass until it cracked. A thin line bled down the middle. Not glass. Not skin. Something between. The candle at the center of the circle guttered, then flared. Sam bowed his head. And from the shadows, something bowed back.

Outside of Time

—The Book Nook sat quietly on the corner of Sycamore and Main, its awning sagging under the weight of time and rain. The hand-painted sign above the door had long since faded, its gold script nearly worn away: The Book Nook — Est. 1974. To anyone else, it might seem an unremarkable relic. But to Donna, it had always been a place outside of time.

Wind chased her down the sidewalk in loose gusts. Leaves, brittle and copper-edged, skittered around her boots. The smell of cinnamon from the bakery two doors down mingled with chimney smoke and dust. The past, waiting.

She paused at the threshold, gloved fingers resting on the worn brass handle. The door creaked as she pushed it open, and the bell overhead chimed once...sharp, clear, and welcoming.

Inside, the Book Nook held steady. Shelves bowed under decades of accumulation; their contents curated like artifacts. The air smelled of paper and wood polish and the lingering trace of Jess Porter's vanilla-spice lotion. Light from the front window cast soft shadows across stacks of fiction and folklore. The fireplace at the back pulsed with a quiet flame, nestled among armchairs that sagged like tired elders.

"Donna!" Jess Caldwell emerged from behind the counter, brushing a wisp of gray hair from her forehead. She navigated the labyrinth of cookbooks and staff picks with ease, pulling Donna into a hug that smelled like vanilla-spice and warmth.

They didn't need to speak. Jess had always been able to read Donna's weather.

"Go on," Jess murmured, nudging her toward the shelves. "Find something to lose yourself in."

Donna drifted through the fiction aisle. Her fingers trailed over familiar spines, the textures grounding her. A title caught her eye...The River Below. She'd read it years ago but couldn't remember a word of it. She opened to the middle and let her eyes scan the page. Something in the rhythm of the language struck a chord.

And then...just for a moment...she remembered.

Not the book. Not the story. But a sound.

A voice, low and layered with age. Speaking words, she didn't understand, but somehow recognized.

She closed her eyes. Let the fire's crackle and the whisper of turning pages fill her ears. Beneath them, under everything, she felt the hum of something stirring. Something old. Something waiting.

She wasn't afraid.

She turned the page.

Chapter 9

Alīesung

Later, Donna was still at The Book Nook continuing her search for a literary escape by wandering down the narrow aisle of The Book Nook, sunlight from the front window tracing golden slivers across the dust motes in the air. She slid her fingers along a shelf of weathered spines until she looked back over her left shoulder at the cart where she had retrieved her first-round subjects. Something that she didn't notice there before...a squat, leather-bound volume. It lay half-hidden under a couple of non-descript books, its cracked cover puckered at the edges. She lifted it and, with the pad of her thumb, traced the raised lettering: faint ridges whispering secrets of centuries past.

She flipped it open to what ought to have been the publication page. Instead of the familiar slickness of modern paper, her palm encountered a rough, grainy surface neither papery nor fibrous, but something like tanned hide. Her pulse quickened. Carefully, she thumbed through the first few pages, scanning blocky lines of ink. No date, no printer's mark...only the bold, single-word title scrawled at the top: "Alīesung." The air in the tiny shop felt suddenly colder. This book wasn't just old; it was ancient.

She leaned closer to read the script, her breath fogging the page. Some words danced in an unfamiliar tongue Old English, Latin, or something else entirely. Then one word pinned her in place: Hayes. She exhaled sharply: "Hayes?!" At that instant, a bolt of memory struck her. The creak of a back door, the metallic tang of fear, her ex-husband Sam's face lit by pale moonlight so vivid it yanked her upright. Her elbow clipped the corner of the wooden table, and a few drops of coffee arced into the air, landing in a dark pool on the floorboards.

"Donna? You okay?" Jess called from behind a sagging counter piled with postcards and knickknacks. The bustling bookseller peeked around a stack of novels; her gray-flecked hair tied in a loose knot. Donna's fingers curled white around the book. Heart hammering, she forced a breath. "Y-yeah. Fine." She pressed her lips together, tasting ash and adrenaline.

Around her, the shop's quiet seemed to swell. Her knees trembled, and she sat on a nearby stool, the leather squeaking beneath her. Memories from last night...her fractured voice, the slam of the front door rose like ghosts. Her jaw clenched until her teeth ground against each other. A hot pulse throbbed at her temples, and her hands, now tightly wound fists, shook so fiercely the book rattled on her lap. Just like before...sudden stillness.

She froze.

The name that had wisped from her lips before, found expression once more ...low and insistent:

What did it mean? Why here? Why now?

When her breathing slowed and the tremors subsided into a dull hum, she stood and tucked her newfound book, Alīesung, under her arm. At the counter, she laid the book beside Jess's half-finished cup of coffee. "Where did this come from?" she asked, voice hushed.

Jess shrugged, fingering a chipped mug. "Came in a box with a bunch of other donations. Don't have a clue who sent 'em."

Donna tapped her foot. "What'll you take for it?"

Jess tilted her head, considering. "No clue on value either. Ten, fifteen...twenty?"

"Twenty's fine." Donna fumbled a crumpled bill from her wallet and pressed it into Jess's palm. "Thanks." She snagged her tote, slung it over her shoulder, and slipped the book inside. With a final nod, she hurried for the door, the bell's jingle trailing behind her as she vanished into the outside world Alīesung clutched tightly against her side, its hidden story now hers to unravel.

What's to Come?

The rain began just after dusk, soft as breath on glass. It tapped against the windows like a reminder. The sky above Redemption Falls had turned the color of old bruises, the kind that never fully faded. Mist drifted in slow tendrils from the hollers, curling low across the fields like it was searching for something…or someone.

Donna stood alone in the living room, the Alīesung resting on the table before her. She hadn't lit the lamps yet. Shadows pressed in at the corners of the room, but she didn't mind them now. The book was open to a page that hadn't been there yesterday…she was sure of it. The ink shimmered faintly in the gloom, the characters not just read but felt, like a song she'd heard as a child and forgotten until now.

Something was changing in her. Or being uncovered.

She sank to the floor, legs folded beneath her, hands hovering over the page like she was afraid to touch it. But she wasn't. Not really. She already had. Over and over. The pages turned in her sleep now. The words whispered when no one else was nearby.

Her mother's voice came to her suddenly, clear and uninvited.

It skips sometimes, but it never forgets. The Circle chooses, even when the one chosen doesn't yet know why.

Donna hadn't known what she meant, back then. A fever dream. A grief-drenched muttering. But now…

Now, the book felt less like an artifact and more like a gate.

She reached for the margin of the page, where a symbol had been scrawled…a looping knot of lines she recognized from the hollow tree behind the Miller house. Her father had called it the "last breath mark." Said it was carved by the first sin eater in their line, meant to hold the weight of what couldn't be spoken aloud.

The old rites had always been spoken of sideways in her family. Half-jokes. Hushed warnings. Prayers disguised as old wives' tales. But now the stories stood up straight, stepped into the room with her, bone and breath and memory.

She traced the symbol with her fingertip.

It pulsed once beneath her skin.

Then the pain came...not sharp, but deep. Like something was burrowing behind her ribs. She gasped and leaned forward; one hand braced against the floor.

She saw faces. Brief, flickering. A girl kneeling in the snow, blackened teeth. A man with ash across his eyes. A circle of twelve, firelit and silent, their palms open to the earth.

Then it was gone.

Donna blinked hard and sat up straighter.

She wasn't losing her mind. Not entirely.

She was remembering something that wasn't hers, not originally. But it had been passed down. Folded into blood and marrow. And now it had arrived at her.

A knock came at the door...three sharp raps, then stillness.

She rose on unsteady feet and opened it.

No one stood there.

Only a bundle wrapped in oilcloth, laid on the porch like an offering.

She brought it inside, unwrapped it slowly. A linen garment, hand-stitched, patterned with the same sigils as the book. Beneath it, a small wooden bowl, charred on one side. And a folded slip of parchment. No name. Just three words, written in the same trembling ink:

You are vessel.

Her hands shook. She pressed the linen to her chest and stood there as the storm finally broke open above Redemption Falls, thunder rolling low across the valley.

The house groaned in the wind, the trees bowing outside as if in recognition.

She turned back to the Alīesung. The new page had vanished.

But the hum remained.

And Donna…rooted now in something far older than fear…no longer doubted what was being asked of her.

She would carry it.

Whatever it was, however, heavy.

She was the vessel.

And the rites would rise again.

Chapter 10

The Call

It was just after nine o'clock when Donna's phone buzzed against the side table, breaking the hush that had settled in the living room. The lamp by the couch threw a warm circle of light onto the hardwood floor, but the rest of the house lay in shadows, listening.

She didn't expect to see Josh's name. For a moment, her thumb hovered over the green icon, heart thudding. Then she answered. "Hey, baby."

"Hey, Mom." Josh's voice was lower than she remembered, a little deeper each time they talked. "Whatchya doin'?" She sank into the corner of the couch, one leg curled under her. "Never too busy for you."

There was a pause, the kind that held more than silence. "You, okay?" she asked.

"Yeah. I just..." He trailed off. In the background, she heard the low rumble of a television, the sound of dishes being stacked. "Is that Michael?" she asked gently. Josh exhaled. "Yeah. He's in the kitchen with Dad. They're doing... something. Trying to make cookies, I think." Donna smiled faintly. "Brave."

Josh chuckled, and just like that, the tension eased. "They're a disaster. Michael dropped a whole egg on the floor and tried to scoop it up with a paper plate."

She could see it, perfectly. His skinny arms, the wild cowlick in the back of his hair, the way he stuck out his tongue when he concentrated. Her throat tightened.

"I miss you guys," she whispered.

Josh didn't say anything for a second.

Then, quietly, "We miss you too." The silence returned…heavier now, like the sky before a storm.

"I talked to Mr. Bookout," she said softly. "The lawyer. We're moving forward. There's still a lot to do, but... we're trying." Josh's voice dropped.

"Dad's mad." "I know." "He doesn't say it. But he is."

"He doesn't have to say it," Donna murmured.

"You've always been good at reading the room." He gave a small laugh, but it didn't last.

"He said you're not stable. That you're... sick." Her stomach twisted.

"Did he say that in front of Michael?"

"No. Just me."

She bit her lip. "You know that's not true, right?"

"I know what I see," Josh said firmly. "You're different from Dad, but that doesn't mean you're wrong. When we're with you... it feels like we're allowed to breathe."

Donna closed her eyes, pain slicing through her chest. "I'm trying, Josh. I really am."

"I know." There was a shuffling sound…then Michael's voice, faint and insistent in the background. Josh muffled the phone.

"Yeah, I'm coming…give me a second!" He came back. "I gotta go."

Donna blinked fast. "Okay."

"But Mom?"

"Yeah, baby?"

"I found the candle." She froze.

"What candle?"

"In the box from last fall. The red one. From the night we went to the old church."

A lump rose in her throat. "You kept that?"

"I keep it under my bed," he said, as if that explained everything.

"Sometimes I light it. Just for a minute. When I miss you." Tears slipped down her cheeks.

"You always said the flame remembers," he added, voice barely above a whisper. "I believe you."

She pressed her fingers to her mouth, too overwhelmed to speak.

"Tell Michael I love him," she finally managed. "I will." "Goodnight, baby." "Night, Mom." The line went dead. Donna held the phone to her chest, heartbeat wild and fractured. Outside, thunder rolled across the sky, soft and distant. But inside her, the storm had already arrived.

Later…

It started with a hum.

Not a mechanical noise…not the refrigerator, not the pipes. No, this was softer. Throat-born. Melodic.

Donna paused mid-step on the trail behind her house, the one that curved just shy of the ridge. A mist clung to the low ground like breath held too long, pale and curling along the edges of the path. The sky had gone silver. The kind of Appalachian dusk where time didn't pass so much as bend.

She clutched her thermos tighter, heart already racing. She hadn't planned to walk far, just enough to clear her head. The boys' voices still echoed in her thoughts from the night before. The candle. The phone call. "The flame remembers." And now, this hum…barely there, but winding into her bones. It came again. Higher now. Childlike. A tune without words, drifting from the trees beyond the bend.

Donna hesitated. She should've turned around. Gone back to the porch. But her feet moved forward, slow, soundless on the soft earth.

She followed the sound down into a narrow hollow. The fog thickened, stirred by something she couldn't see. Her breath hitched.

That's when she saw her. A girl stood just beyond the tree line…barefoot, pale, maybe ten years old. Hair the color of storm-soaked straw hung down her back. She wore a faded white dress that clung to her like river moss. Her head was tilted slightly, as if listening to something even deeper in the woods.

Donna froze. The girl was humming. The same tune. Then, without a word or a glance, she turned and walked deeper into the trees. Her feet didn't disturb the leaves. Donna stepped forward, but the fog thickened instantly, swallowing the girl's silhouette like a tide coming in.

"Hello?" Donna called, voice barely above a whisper. "Are you lost?"

No answer. Only that melody... trailing off like breath on glass.

The silence that followed wasn't empty. It was full. Watching. She stood for a moment more, heart thudding in her throat, then turned and stumbled back toward home. Her hands shook as she unlocked the back door. Once inside, she leaned against the counter, listening for the sound again. But it was gone. And outside, the mist had vanished like it had never been there. _____

That night, sleep wouldn't come. In the stillness, Donna lit a lone candle on the desk, its flame trembling against the dark. She opened Alīesung, the paper cool beneath her fingertips, and let the book fall open to where her reading had last been abandoned.

Something in her resisted moving too far, too fast. But now... she flipped to a page she hadn't marked.

The ink was browner here, older maybe. Faded. The page bore no heading, just a single, narrow entry:

"She came again in the fog. The child with the owl's voice. She hums the memory of the undone. Grandmother says she is the shape of unburied sin...the ones too small to name, the ones left behind by those too proud to claim them. She walks the edge of the veil, calling out not with words, but with songs we almost remember. The women of the ridge leave her milk and silver thistle, lest she follow them home." Donna stared at the passage, blood cold in her limbs. Milk. And silver thistle. She didn't know what silver thistle was. But she'd kept goat's milk in the fridge ever since Josh's stomach issues started. She looked toward the back door. The woods beyond stood still. But in her ears, faint and sudden, the melody returned.

Just for a moment. Then silence. And Donna whispered into the dark, "I see you."

Chapter 11

Breakfast and Redemption

Beau pushed open the chipped motel door and squinted against the low morning sun as it struck the peeling paint.

He crossed the gravel parking lot, each step crunching beneath his worn boots, unlocked the driver's side of his black SUV, and tossed his duffel bag onto the passenger seat. The engine coughed to life, but he left it idling. Atlanta could wait. He cracked the window and breathed in cool air tinged with woodsmoke, maybe someone's backyard fire. His stomach growled. Breakfast first.

He eased onto Main Street, gravel giving way to cracked asphalt. Storefronts lined the road: a faded barber pole next to a boarded-up theater, a hardware store with dusty windows, then Momma's on Main Street. The turquoise sign, its cursive letters curling like old lace, promised eggs cooked fresh and coffee strong enough to chase ghosts away. He parked between a rust-speckled mail truck and a burgundy sedan, grabbed his keys, and stepped onto the sun-warmed sidewalk.

Inside, a bell tinkled overhead and the scent of butter sizzling in a cast-iron skillet rolled through the air. Sunlight filtered through lace-trimmed curtains, dust motes drifting over red-checked tablecloths. Walls were plastered with yellowed newspaper clippings and sepia photographs of fishing derbies and football teams from decades past. A row of cracked vinyl booths hugged the wall; a gleaming chrome counter with red stools ran the length of the room. Beau approached just as a slender woman with streaked gray hair and flour-smudged apron called from the kitchen pass-through, "Sit wherever ya like, hon."

He slid into a booth by the window, angling his back to the wall so he could see the door...old habits die hard. The woman, nametag reading "Luanne," wiped her hands on her apron and hovered beside him, pen poised over a small pad. Lines fanned from her tired eyes, but her smile was easy. Beau leaned forward. "How're your pancakes?" he asked. She nodded confidently. "Better than any you'll git down the road, sweetie." He ordered two fluffy buttermilk pancakes, bacon crisp enough to snap, eggs over easy, and black coffee. Luanne snatched a steaming mug from the counter and set it before him. He wrapped both hands around it, welcoming the warmth, and inhaled deeply.

Out the window, a trio of kids pedaled by on squeaky bikes. A woman in a sunhat talked over a crate of tomatoes with a man in overalls. Their easy laughter drifted in, a soundtrack of ordinary life. Beau's shoulders, usually coiled like springs, relaxed for the first time in weeks.

Luanne returned with his plate moments later. The pancakes were golden-brown, edges crisp; bacon curled like crimson ribbons; eggs glowed buttercup-yellow. He cut into the stack, watching steam spiral skyward, and let the first bite melt on his tongue. Simple sweetness. No alarms, no contracts pending, no ghosts on the horizon, just honest food in a room frozen in time.

As locals drifted in tipping their hats, ordering hashbrowns or gravy-smothered biscuits, Beau studied them. They laughed at inside jokes, leaned back in chairs, sighed over bills paid. What would it be like to wake up here every day without a plan to run? He closed his eyes, spoon hovering above his coffee, and let a quiet longing settle in his chest. Maybe redemption wasn't a distant myth. Maybe it started right here.

-------------------- Beau continued sipping his coffee while gazing out the window onto Main Street, but the warmth didn't reach his chest anymore. It sat heavy in his stomach like a stone, anchoring him to something he didn't want to remember.

The syrup on his plate glistened under the sunlight, amber and innocent, but his eyes had already drifted, beyond the red-checked tablecloth, beyond Luanne's soft humming, beyond the easy rhythm of a town that didn't know his name. His gaze fell on the chrome napkin holder, warped slightly, and in its sheen, he saw something else.

He saw a motel...just like the one he stayed in last night...years ago. Louisiana, maybe. Or Arkansas. It didn't matter. They all blurred now.

The air had been wet with summer heat. Cicadas screamed from the trees. He remembered the metallic sting of sweat in his eyes and the way his finger trembled on the trigger even though his voice had been steady.

The man's name had been Martin Brewer. Low-level debt runner. Ex-military. A burner phone and a reputation for talking too much. Beau had been promised it'd be clean, quick. No family, no complications. Just a hotel room, a key card slid under the door, and a duffel full of untraceable bills waiting at the end.

He remembered the knock.

Not the shot, not first. That came later. It was the knock that stuck with him...the way Martin opened the door, blinking like he'd just come from sleep, confused but not afraid. Like Beau might've been someone else. A friend. A mistake.

Then came the weight of the silenced pistol in his hand.

And the moment...the half-second...when Martin realized.

"Wait..." he'd said.

That was all.

A flash. A muffled pop. A red bloom on a threadbare motel curtain. Beau stood there, gun still raised, as the man crumpled like a broken chair.

Martin didn't scream. Didn't fight. He just looked up at Beau with the barest expression of betrayal, like he'd expected better from the world.

Beau remembered stepping back, barely breathing. The air smelled of mildew and burnt gunpowder. The carpet was sticky beneath his boots. He hadn't eaten that day, and afterward, when he tried, everything tasted like ash.

Back in the diner, a fork clattered to the floor, jolting Beau from the memory. He blinked; throat tight. His coffee had gone cold.

"Y'okay, sugar?" Luanne's voice floated over like a raft.

Beau looked up slowly. "Yeah," he said, the lie smooth and practiced. "Just tired."

She gave him a knowing smile and moved on to the next table, calling someone "darlin'" as she poured more coffee.

But Beau's hands had started to tremble.

He clenched them in his lap.

Martin had a daughter. Beau found out a month later...barely a mention in a folder during another job, just a name and a birthday scribbled on a wrinkled receipt in Martin's wallet.

The guilt had settled then, quiet and suffocating, like vines creeping over a house.

He looked around the diner, at the old men arguing over baseball, at the smell of home-fried potatoes and the scrape of forks on ceramic plates.

Maybe there was still time...Atlanta could wait a little longer.

Maybe redemption didn't come all at once. Maybe it came in moments.

Ron Day

Chapter 12

The Waking Grove

Donna stood at the edge of the kitchen table, the old book still in her hands, spine creaking slightly as if resisting being opened again. Alīesung. The name had curled itself around her thoughts like a vine, dragging pieces of memory up from dark soil. The air in the house had changed since she brought the book home…too still, too quiet. Even the ticking of the wall clock felt muffled, like sound had to fight its way through.

She should have gone to bed. Should have checked in with Dan. Should have locked the doors and told herself stories about tomorrow. Instead, she sat cross-legged on the rug beside the fireplace, the book resting in her lap, a candle burning low on the hearth.

Her thumb skimmed a page with a faded sigil, and her vision blurred…not from tears or exhaustion, but from something deeper. Like the air had shifted again, the room pulling away like a tide. She didn't fall asleep. That much she would swear to later. But she blinked…and she was in the grove.

The trees here were older than any map, their trunks wide as vault doors, bark twisted with the patience of centuries. Moss curled upward along the roots like hands frozen mid-prayer. The air smelled of damp ash and something sweet honeysuckle maybe, or decay. Light didn't seem to come from above, but from the mist itself, a silver-gray haze that glowed softly around the clearing.

In the center stood a circle of standing stones, each carved with faint symbols nearly rubbed away by time. Her bare feet stepped silently across the mossy ground. She felt no wind. No cold. Only a thrumming...like a heartbeat in the dirt. Something called her forward. Not in words. Not even sound. But presence.

At the edge of the stones, Donna hesitated. One of them, slightly taller than the rest, was slick with something dark. Not blood. Not exactly. More like shadow made liquid. Her breath hitched. She reached out and pressed her palm to the stone. Heat flared beneath her skin. Then came the vision.

A young woman, barefoot in a nightdress, kneeling in this same grove. Her hair was wild, and her arms outstretched. Flames encircled her...small, con-trolled, as if tamed by will alone. Surrounding her, a dozen others, faces obscured by hoods, chanted words Donna couldn't understand. The woman cried out...not in fear but power. Her back arched. Her mouth opened and light poured from her eyes.

Donna gasped and stepped back. Her hand left the stone and the vision broke. The grove shimmered again, dimming at the edges. Then, she heard a whisper. Not from the trees. Not from the wind. From the earth itself.

"You carry what he could not."

Donna turned, heart hammering. "Who?" The ground pulsed once beneath her feet. From behind the largest tree, a figure stepped out…long coat, eyes hidden beneath a wide-brimmed hat. His outline shimmered, half-real, like he was stitched from breath and smoke.

"Blood remembers," he said, voice low, ragged with centuries. "You think the sins stay buried because you stopped speaking their names?"

Donna couldn't move. Could barely breathe. Her voice scraped its way out. "What... do you want?" He tilted his head.

"To warn you." Lightning forked across the mist, silent and brilliant. For a moment, the grove was etched in silver light. Then the shadows closed again. "They'll come for the book. But the book is not what they fear."

"What, then?" she asked.

The figure leaned close. His breath chilled her cheek.

"You." She jerked backward and opened her eyes on her living room floor. The candle had burned to a nub. The fire was out. The room smelled of wax and smoke. Her hand still rested on the cover of Alīesung, the imprint of the sigil pressed faintly into her skin like an inkless brand. Outside, a crow cawed once, sharp and distant.

Donna rose on unsteady legs and moved toward the sink. Her hands trembled under the faucet. As she splashed her face, she caught her reflection in the window above the basin…her eyes wide, skin pale. And behind her, for just a second, the faint outline of a man in a wide-brimmed hat. When she spun, the kitchen was empty. But the air still hummed.

Chapter 13

The Last Rite of Josiah Walker

The page feels warm beneath her fingertips. Donna isn't sure if it's her imagination or the book itself. The script is old, uneven, written in an ink that has browned like blood left in sunlight. There are no headings, only a faint symbol pressed into the corner: a looped sigil that hums faintly in the edge of her vision if she stares too long.

The passage begins without explanation.

_____Redemption Falls, 1874

Snow fell sideways the night Josiah Walker died, blanketing the high ridges in silence thick as sorrow. He was laid out on the parlor table, arms crossed in solemn surrender, his boots still flecked with coal dust and his jaw set in stone. The old ways said a sin-eater couldn't be buried until the weight he carried was passed on. And Josiah had carried more than most.

He had been the Walker of Sins since 1832, when his brother died screaming with no one to claim his transgressions. Josiah was nineteen then, raw-boned and angry, full of fire and hunger. They said he took the bread and salt without flinching and never spoke of the shadows he saw afterward.

Now, forty-two years later, Redemption Falls stood on the edge of forgetting again.

And the rite could not go undone.

They brought him up Black Hollow Ridge just after midnight, six kin in dark coats, their breath rising in mist. No preacher came. This was older than scripture. Older than language.

They laid Josiah atop the stone circle. A crust of bread rested on his chest. A bowl of salt at his feet. Candles flickered against the wind, flames curving toward the trees like they wanted to flee.

And from the darkness, Asa Walker came.

His boots cracked frozen moss, his coat slick with snowmelt. He had not been seen in Redemption Falls for nearly six winters. When he left, he had sworn a vow never to return…not while Ruth still lived, not while Josiah still breathed. But death has a way of calling back what life cannot.

He knelt beside the body.

"Name the sins," he said.

Ruth's voice trembled as she spoke, reading from a ledger older than any living soul.

Wrath against a preacher who buried a child without the rite.

Envy toward a neighbor with unblighted land.

Pride in keeping the secrets others feared.

And the worst of all...silence when he should have spoken.

With each word, Asa ate a bite of the bread. His face twisted, but he did not stop.

When the bread was gone, he took the salt into his hand, held it to the sky, and whispered in a language none remembered...but all feared.

Then he scattered it across Josiah's chest.

The wind rose.

And with it, something else.

Asa's body convulsed. His spine arched, eyes rolling white. A sound escaped him...not a scream, not a groan, but a shudder of the earth itself. Those watching did not move. To interrupt was to inherit the curse.

When it passed, Asa fell forward on his knees. Steam lifted from his skin. His breath came in broken bursts.

"It is done," he rasped.

Someone offered water. He waved it away. Instead, his eyes turned to the youngest girl watching from the tree line.

Mercy Walker.

He looked at her long.

"Next time," he whispered, "it'll be you."

Then he rose and was gone.

They buried Josiah before the sun broke the ridge. No sermon. No stone.

Just packed earth and wind.

But days later, Mercy returned to the circle. The snow had melted in patches where the salt had landed.

And beside it...

Hoofprints. Not horse. Not deer. Spaced too far apart.

No tracks leading in. No tracks leading out.

Just the mark of something watching.

Something called by name.

Donna's finger pauses on the final sentence. She feels the air around her change.

The room smells faintly of burned cedar.

And in her spine, a cold bloom of recognition:

Mercy Walker.

She's seen that name before...

on her mother's birth certificate.

A tremor moves through her.

She turns the page.

Chapter 14

The Break In

The first sound that woke her was the breaking of glass...not loud, it took Jess a while to come to...and then it was the whisper of paper. A soft shush, like pages being turned by hands too impatient for silence. Jess bolted upright on the threadbare velvet couch in the shop's back corner, still tangled in her quilt.

She hadn't meant to fall asleep here, not again, but the autumn thunderstorm rolling over Redemption Falls had lulled her under. Now the air was thick with that unrelenting...charged, expectant.

She stayed still, letting her breath slow. Listening.

There it was again.

Movement.

Not rats. Not wind. Intentional.

She slipped barefoot down the narrow aisle between shelves, each step practiced, careful not to betray her. The Book Nook sighed around her...old wood, old ghosts. The front door hadn't splintered or chimed. Whoever was here had been here before. Knew where to walk.

Near the occult shelf, a figure knelt, flashlight off, working by the dim glow from the streetlamp filtering through stained glass. Broad shoulders. Familiar slouch.

Jess's pulse jumped.

Sam Hayes.

Of course it was.

She edged closer, keeping a table between them. He was flipping through a leather-bound volume, one from the locked cabinet...Alchemical Tongues: A Catalogue of Veiled Names. She could see his lips moving as he read, silently mouthing something like a prayer, or a spell. His fingers trembled...not from fear, but urgency.

Jess felt it like a certainty, rooted in her gut. This wasn't about burglary. This was obsession.

"Looking for something specific?" she said, voice low, calm as river fog.

The figure spun away and ran. Slamming into the old oak bookshelves. Books crashed from the shelf as he lunged sideways, a scatter of brittle pages and dust falling like leaves in his wake. Jess flinched, one hand flying up instinctively as a spine clipped her shoulder. The scent of mildew and iron filled the air as a volume landed at her feet, split wide open like a wounded bird.

By the time she reached the front window, he was gone...just a shadow cutting through the rain, swallowed by the alley's waiting dark.

Jess let the silence settle, broken only by the storm's distant grumble and the slow drip of water from the broken transom. Her breath came hard, not from fear, but from the sudden hollowness his absence left behind. That kind of desperation didn't end when a man ran. It just found new corners to rot in.

She sank to her knees beside the fallen books, as though seeking absolution. Her fingers brushed spines and paper, the chaos of it oddly reverent, until she saw it...an envelope, yellowed with time, wedged between the pages of Liturgy of the Hollow Saints. The flap was unsealed, edges curling like it had been waiting to be found.

Her name was on the front. Not hers. Donna's.

In ink that had softened with age, still legible in the flickering light: To my Donna - when you begin to remember. Granny Ada.

Jess held her breath as she slid the letter free, heart thudding now not with fear, but with something deeper recognition, maybe. Destiny, maybe.

The handwriting inside was strong, deliberate. A voice speaking from beyond the veil.

"Child,

If this letter finds you, then what I feared has begun to stir. You may not recall the old rites, nor the price paid in blood and silence, but they are stitched into your marrow. The sin eaters kept balance…not just of soul, but of all that lies beneath. When one forgets, the veil begins to fray. When all forget…well. The hunger beneath remembers.

This world isn't built to hold back what we buried. And if it rises, it won't come as flame or flood. It'll come as shadow that knows your name.

Forgive me, Donna. I prayed you'd never have to know. But I see now…I was only ever delaying the storm.

When it comes, you'll have to choose. Be the last of us…or be the first."

Jess read it twice, the thunder outside matching the tremor in her chest. She looked toward the door, where rain now veiled the night like a shroud.

She didn't know what Donna would do with this.

But she knew one thing: the past had just come looking.

And it had found its way in.

Donna sat at the kitchen table, Aliesung lying before her like a sealed door she wasn't sure she wanted to open.

The book was wrapped in worn, hand-stitched leather, soft at the edges, as though it had been passed from many hands…some gentle, some trembling. Its title was pressed into the cover in faded gold: Aliesung. No subtitle. No author. Just that one strange, musical word.

The kettle had gone cold. Her tea was untouched. She'd brought the book home from the Book Nook with a knot in her stomach that hadn't uncoiled since she handed Jess that crumpled twenty-dollar bill.

Donna wasn't ready. Not even close.

She had spent the first hour walking around it like it was a spider in the room…too big to ignore, too unnerving to touch. Her thoughts swirled like ash on wind: This is ridiculous. It's just a book. There's nothing in here that hasn't already been lost. And yet, the weight of it…its silence…was unbearable.

She stood now, pacing the kitchen floor in socked feet, arms crossed tight to hold in whatever was trying to shake loose. The tile felt cool, grounding. Outside, the pines of Redemption Falls sighed in the wind, a thousand whispering voices just out of reach.

Why now? she thought. Why me?

A sharp gust hit the window, and the noise it made was like a voice breaking through water. Donna froze, hand gripping the back of a chair.

Something inside her twisted.

She sat again. Her hand hovered above the book. Then, as if someone else guided her, she opened it again.

A faint line of script...handwritten in an ink that shimmered faintly green in the light...appeared like breath fogging on glass:

"To remember is to return. Begin there."

Her breath caught. She touched the words with her fingertips. The ink tingled. Her chest tightened.

"No," she whispered aloud, pulling her hand back. "I don't want this. I didn't ask for this."

And it was true. The grief, the fractures in memory, the strange dreams, the feeling that the woods knew her name...all of it had built a case for madness. And now this book. This invitation.

She stood up too quickly, knocking over her chair. The sound cracked through the house. She pressed her back against the wall, breathing hard, tears threatening.

"I'm not who they think I am," she said aloud, voice trembling. "I'm just Donna. I'm no keeper. No vessel."

But the book stayed open. Still. Waiting.

Outside, a wind chime sang a melody she'd never noticed before. Minor, haunting. Familiar.

Her knees gave out slowly. She slid to the floor, knees tucked to her chest, eyes still on the book.

Donna sobbed once, hard. She didn't understand where the tears came from, only that they came with the sudden realization that her confusion had always been a shield. That the not-knowing had protected her from the truth...the one now uncoiling in her marrow.

She crawled toward the book. Sat before it as though she were about to pray.

"I'm scared," she said to no one, to everyone, to the old rites echoing through the veil of her bloodline.

The book's pages rustled though no wind stirred them. Another page turned on its own.

She didn't fight this time.

What met her eyes wasn't text, but images...drawings of women in ceremony, of circles under starlight, of a forest with trees that bowed toward a hidden center.

She gasped.

In the corner of one page was a small sketch: a young girl kneeling by a river, arms outstretched to something unseen.

Donna remembered that river.

She remembered her.

And in that moment, the confusion didn't vanish...it shifted. Became softer. Not a fog to fear, but a veil to draw back. Something sacred had waited long and quiet inside her. Not demanding. Not loud. But patient.

Donna reached for the book again, this time with no shaking in her hands.

"Okay," she said. "I'll remember."

She needed control. Any control.

Even this.

The pages breathed out the scent of mildew and dust, but beneath it lingered something else...sweet, familiar. Her fingers slowed over a faint smudge in the margin, like a fingerprint left in ash.

She didn't remember ever reading this book. But she knew the rhythm of the words before she turned the page. The language didn't feel learned...it felt remembered, as if some deep part of her had been waiting for it all along.

And there it was: tucked between brittle pages and hand-scrawled margins, a rite. Marked by a symbol she couldn't identify. Words she somehow knew were meant for her.

She should have closed the book. Walked away.

But fear had long since hollowed her out. And the weight of helplessness had worn her down to the bone.

Being afraid all the time and fighting to keep a grip on her mental health had become more unbearable than whatever might happen next.

The instructions were deceptively simple.

Donna picked up the book and walked out the back door of her house...

She struck a match. It hissed to life, the flame sharp and golden.

Donna knelt on the broken stone patio behind the house, her knees pressing into cold moss. October's breath clung to her skin, her fingers stiff and red...not just from the cold, but from the gravity of what she was about to do.

She exhaled. Her breath spilled out in a silvery stream...not quite smoke, not quite fog...lifting from her mouth like a veil drawn back.

She whispered the first line.

And the wind stopped listening.

In front of her sat a shallow bowl of water, its surface smooth and still under the fading light. The bowl had once belonged to her grandmother...stoneware, pale and speckled, with hairline cracks like veins across its surface. Donna remembered it from childhood, always tucked high on a shelf, more relic than dish. Never touched. Never explained.

Tonight, it felt heavier than clay...heavy with memory. Heavy with something waiting.

To her right, a bundle of white sage smoldered in a chipped clay bowl. It, too, might've been her grandmother's. She wasn't sure. The smoke didn't rise straight. It spiraled, drawn by something unseen.

Her back was to the house. To the world. Behind her, the porch light clicked off, casting the patio into bruised twilight.

The quiet that followed was too complete.

Too whole.

Aliesung lay in her lap.

Its leather cover was older than it had any right to be...warm, like skin still holding a breath. It was hers now. That much felt certain. The marked page crackled beneath her thumb; its edges singed from the candles of generations past.

The rite waited.

The words weren't English. Not quite. And not Latin either, though some syllables echoed that forgotten tongue. For Donna, speaking them wasn't like reading...it was like being reminded. The book wasn't teaching her. It was remembering with her.

She drew in a breath.

Felt it catch, then settle. A thread pulled taut.

She struck another match.

The flame leapt up again, hungry. It kissed the tip of the sage bundle, and fire threaded through the leaves in jagged orange veins. Smoke rose, curling around her hands, weaving through the air...clinging to her coat like a shadow finding its form.

She closed her eyes.

"Joshua. Michael," she whispered.

The names snagged in her throat.

Not because of grief...though her chest ached...but because the air pushed back against them, thick as syrup.

As if the names themselves didn't want to be said. As if something had laid claim to them.

"Joshua. Michael," she tried again, voice stronger. "I offer this in your protection."

The fire narrowed. A needle-thin blue-white flame hovered above the sage.

The water in the bowl quivered. A ripple spread outward as if something below had stirred, unseen and immense...suddenly the bowl rattled faintly against the stone...just once...but it was enough.

Her pulse quickened. Her skin tingled. The wind didn't rise, but something around her moved, something the body noticed before the mind could register.

Still, she continued.

She reached into her coat pocket and drew out a folded paper...just one page, torn from a legal packet. It was the court's summary ruling from her first custody hearing. The words blurred even before the flame touched it. She held it above the bowl.

"Burn the fear."

The fire caught fast. Paper curled black and orange. She let it drop, watched it twist like a dying insect, consumed in seconds.

Then it began.

The wind stopped.

Not slowed...stopped. Even the trees, which had been gently swaying in the cold, went rigid. Every chirp, every rustle, every distant hum from the street died at once.

The air pressed down on her shoulders with invisible hands. Her ears rang. A fever heat washed over her, too hot to be natural. Not fire heat. Not flesh heat.

This was the heat of prophecy. Of wrongness. Of memory being pried open.

Her breath hitched.

Then came the voice.

Not outside. Not in her ears.

Inside her skull.

"The door..."

Donna's mouth opened to scream, but her voice betrayed her. No sound came. The bowl of water lifted from the ground for half a second and clattered back down. The bowl cracked along its base. And just as quickly as it began, everything...shifted.

She was no longer on the patio.

She was standing in a field, barefoot in a white linen gown soaked to the knees with something red. But not blood. Not entirely. Her fingers were streaked with ash. Around her, a circle of figures in cloaks knelt in the grass, their heads bowed. A stone altar stood at the center; its surface carved with the same runes from Alīesung. Smoke rose from the edges. Something had just been burned. Something alive.

A woman's voice...her own voice, younger, stronger...spoke from inside her throat.

"Let this blood bind, let this fire cleanse. What was taken shall be restored."

The figures raised their heads.

One wore her father's face.

One, her grandmother's.

One was faceless entirely.

The altar cracked open like dry earth, and from the smoke rose the silhouette of a child...no older than six. His eyes glowed faintly, like embers beneath skin. He raised one hand toward her, then dissolved into ash.

Donna screamed.

The vision broke.

She woke in bed, drenched in sweat, mouth open, throat dry.

The window beside her was open. The wind tugged at the curtain like a whispering hand. Her jeans were still on. One sock missing. Her soles smeared with dried mud. Her coat lay crumpled in the doorway like she'd thrown it from across the room.

The book Alïesung sat neatly on the dresser, closed. A black feather...too long, too perfect...was tucked into the pages like a bookmark.

She didn't own anything with feathers.

Her phone vibrated on the nightstand. A voicemail from Dan. Timestamp: 1:17 a.m.

She sat frozen until the screen went dark.

Then, slowly, she stood and crossed to the vanity mirror. Flicked on the light.

Bloodshot eyes. Dirt on her cheek. Ash under her fingernails. The bowl with a brand hairline crack to add to the others.

The circle hadn't sealed.

The rite hadn't ended.

It had only just begun.

And something...something older than Redemption Falls, older than her blood...was watching.

Chapter 15

The Sorrow of Asa Walker

Donna felt it before she named it: that subtle tug low in her ribs, like the hush before a summer storm. She needed to go to Momma's on Main Street. Not a thought, not even a decision...just a knowing. She would have to stop there.

She washed the ash from her hands, scrubbed the dirt from her face until her skin stung, and twisted her hair back with trembling fingers. Her boots were already by the door. She was halfway across the living room when something made her stop.

Alīesung.

It lay open on the kitchen table, pages curled slightly at the edges as if breathing.

Donna turned toward it.

The heading on the exposed page struck like a whisper straight to her spine:

_____Redemption Falls, 1874

As transcribed from the final entry in Alīesung

Snow had long since covered the trail behind him, but Asa Walker didn't look back. The cold burned his lungs with every breath, a sharp reminder that he was still, regrettably, alive. Wind cut through the gaps in his wool coat as he stepped over the last ridge and caught sight of the hollow where the stone circle lay buried under the whitening dark.

He'd told himself he wouldn't come back. Six winters away should've been enough. Enough to drown

Ruth's memory, enough to shake Josiah's name from his spine. But then the telegram came, short and cruel:

He's dead. They've laid him out for the rite.

No signature. No mercy.

And so here he was, boots sinking into snow so thick the world seemed silent but for the hammering of his heart.

The others...kin and not...stood in black around Josiah's still form, their faces hollowed by candlelight. Salt crusted in a bowl at his feet, and a crust of bread sat square atop his chest. Asa's mouth went dry.

"Name the sins," he said, throat raw.

They did. Ruth's voice most of all. Trembling but clear.

As each sin was spoken...wrath, envy, silence...Asa ate. He chewed the bread until it turned bitter and dry as ash. He swallowed and swallowed again, though it fought to stay down. And when it was done, he scattered the salt across Josiah's chest and whispered the old words...words he barely remembered learning, words that felt like hot iron poured down the throat.

The wind moaned like a warning. And then the pain began.

His knees buckled as something cracked open inside him…like a rib splitting, only deeper. He saw things behind his eyelids: a woman weeping blood in a house with no roof, a child buried in tree roots, a crow-faced man with no shadow leaning over Josiah's still mouth. Each vision struck like lightning. Not thoughts. Not memories. Echoes. Guilt not his, sin not his, grafted into bone.

When it was over, Asa lay on the stones, steaming in the cold, his mouth open to the stars. He felt emptied…but not clean.

He returned to his mother's house by the river, silent as a ghost. Weeks passed. The others went back to church and chores, the way folk always did after a death, as if the darkness had passed.

But Asa knew better.

The sins never truly left. They took up residence…in the hollow of the chest, behind the eyes. They watched.

It began with the mark.

A line of black beneath his collarbone, raised and jagged like a burn. It itched some nights, throbbed others. Sometimes, in the dark, it pulsed. He caught it glowing faintly once in the washbasin, like embers left too long in a hearth.

Then came the crows.

They followed him…perched on rooftops, power lines, chimney stacks. Never calling. Just watching. One morning he opened his door and found one on the threshold, wings outstretched. Dead, but upright, balanced like a sentinel.

At first, he thought madness. But the mirror said otherwise. When he looked into his own eyes, he saw Josiah staring back.

He kept to himself after that.

He stopped speaking at church, skipped the town fairs, answered only when pressed. They called him strange. Cursed. Some whispered he'd murdered Josiah and eaten the sin by force. He let them talk.

The only thing that brought him comfort was the book.

Bound in old leather, passed down from sin-eater to sin-eater. Alīesung. The record of rites, visions, warnings. He wrote in it when the dreams came too strong, when the voices began to rise at night, whispering things he dared not repeat.

Let the next one know, he wrote. Let them read this before they kneel.

The mark spread by the third month…now shaped like a looped branch. It hurt when he lied. It burned when someone nearby sinned. The townsfolk thought him a prophet, a madman, or both. A child once touched his hand and wept for no reason.

He began wearing gloves.

Tonight, Asa sits at the desk beneath the oil lamp. It flickers once, twice, casting shadows that slither instead of stretch. He knows the time is near.

He has heard the sound again…that deep tolling bell from the woods, the one only the marked can hear. The same sound that rang in Josiah's last hour.

He dips the pen.

To the one who inherits this...

Know the bread tastes of ash.

Know the salt remembers.

The mark will find you. In dreams, or blood, or breath.

And when it does, do not run. The ridge will call you home.

He stops. The lamp gutters. Somewhere beyond the window, the crows stir.

A final line:

I carried the sins of Josiah Walker. And maybe some of yours too.

Asa closes the book.

And from somewhere in the holler, beneath roots and stone, something hums in reply.

---------Donna was reeling from the entry. Her shoulders tightened as she sat at the kitchen table.

Finally, she was up and moving toward the front door...a quick stop at Bookout Family Law and then on to Momma's on Main Street.

Chapter 16

Choose Your Weapons

Donna's hand hovered just short of the paper.

The folder sat open between them...cream-colored, clinical, and sharp-edged. A name in bold at the top of the page:

Retainer Agreement – Client: Donna Miller

It could have said: This is how the war begins.

Scott nudged the document closer with a single fingertip, as if nudging it too hard might set something off.

A light knock at the doorframe. Sylvia entered, her shoes whispering across the carpet. She held two additional pages like they were church relics...reverent, detached, practiced. The kind of woman who could carry a confession and never flinch.

"Standard disclosures," she said, her voice low.

"And a financial summary. If anything doesn't read right, just flag me."

"Thanks, Sylvia," Scott murmured, not lifting his eyes.

Donna didn't speak. Just nodded, and that was enough.

The door clicked softly behind Sylvia.

Then...silence.

Not empty silence, but the kind that settles after the last hymn, or after a body's been taken out of the room and the air forgets how to breathe.

Donna picked up the pen.

It was silver. Real silver, by the look and the weight of it. Balanced. Heavy like old promises. It fit into her hand as if it had been waiting there.

Her fingers curled around it. The tip hovered.

She stared at the blank line beneath her name.

"I can't undo what's already happened," she said quietly.

Scott nodded once. "No. But you can choose what happens next."

She signed.

The first letter faltered. A stammer in ink. D for Donna …drawn too sharply.

By the end of Miller, her hand had steadied, but the pen lingered too long. A single drop of ink welled and fell.

It landed like a bruise.

She blinked down at it.

"You okay?" Scott asked, his voice stripped of its lawyer-tone. Just a man in a quiet room.

There was a sound.

Behind her.

A soft, persistent tapping…tick... tick... tick...

She turned.

A fly was battering its body against the windowpane. Large. Off-color. Moving wrong. Its wings buzzed a low, teeth-itching rhythm as it slammed again and again into the glass, determined to break through.

Donna stood. She grabbed a folder from the corner of the desk and swatted once, hard.

A sharp snap.

The thing dropped out of sight.

She stayed there a moment too long, staring out the window. The sky looked normal. Trees bowing in the breeze. An old paper sign taped to a telephone pole that read CHURCH BBQ SAT 4PM. Nothing out of place.

And yet…

She turned back. "Sorry."

"No need," Scott said, reaching for the second page. "Most pests around here take more than one swat."

Donna gave him a small smile, the kind that never reaches the eyes.

She signed again. This time, her hand didn't shake.

Scott nodded, collected the papers, and slid them into a folder before locking the drawer with a quiet click.

"That's the easy part," he said. "The next steps aren't."

"I know."

"You'll need documentation. Testimony, maybe. Medical records, psychological evaluations. Character witnesses…friends, family, partner."

Donna winced.

Scott caught it.

"You mentioned someone. Dan?"

"Yes." She swallowed. "He's good. He's not part of this."

Scott didn't argue. Just leaned back in his chair.

"Good people get pulled under all the same."

He stood, straightened his sleeves. "I'll start the petition. Custody modification, updated evaluations, access to the transcripts and the hospital logs."

"I've got the logs," she said. "And the transcripts. In a box I couldn't bring myself to throw away."

"Then we're ahead," he said.

He clicked the pen once before setting it in its tray.

Donna looked down.

The drop of ink hadn't dried.

It still sat there, gleaming. A little too dark.

Scott walked her to the door. Formal, polite. But his eyes lingered…not unkind, just careful. Like someone who'd once opened a cabinet and found something moving where nothing should move.

Donna felt the weight of that stare between her shoulder blades, even after he turned away.

"Thank you," she said at the threshold.

"We'll be in touch by Friday. But if anything changes…if Sam shows up, or if you feel threatened…call."

His voice was steady, but something had slipped. A thread pulled loose.

She didn't ask.

She didn't want to know what he'd seen in her.

Out in the reception area, Sylvia rose halfway and handed her a printout.

"Your copy," she said gently. "And... good luck, Mrs. Miller."

Donna nodded.

The glass door let out a soft whine as she stepped through.

Outside, the wind had shifted.

It wasn't colder. Just... hollower. As if something had moved out of the air and left a space behind.

Shadows pooled differently now. Edges sharper.

Her car waited at the far end of the lot… dusty, blue, alone.

She crossed the gravel. Each step cracked dry pebbles beneath her boots. A dog barked in the distance. Then cut off too quick.

She stopped.

Looked up.

Across the street, under the skeletal sprawl of a half-dead sycamore, stood a man.

Tall. Still.

He wore a long coat that didn't shift in the wind. A hat, brim low. His shape wavered... like heat rising off blacktop.

Donna squinted.

She couldn't see his face.

But she knew he was watching.

A car passed. A blur of movement.

When it was gone, the sidewalk was empty.

Just air.

Just absence.

She reached her car, slid into the driver's seat, and pulled the door shut.

Her hands shook on the steering wheel. The papers Sylvia had given her was still clenched tight.

She stared through the windshield. The sky looked the same. But she knew better.

"You started this," she whispered. "So, finish it."

The key turned.

The engine caught.

The dash clock blinked to life: 9:00 AM

Exactly.

Like a mark.

Like a warning.

Like something was watching the time.

Chapter 17

The Pastor's Secret

He hadn't been Pastor Jim back then.

Just Jim.

The year was 1989, and summer had bled into October too fast. The hills had turned brittle gold, the skies the color of old ash. He was twenty-three, fresh out of seminary and only two months into his new calling...the pulpit passed down by his father, who was dying slower than anyone wanted to admit.

It was a Friday night when the boy disappeared. Eli Candler, age eleven. Last seen playing by the creek behind the parsonage just before dusk. His mother had only turned her back to stir stew on the stove.

They searched all night, calling his name into the wind. The sheriff brought dogs, and half the town joined in... boots in wet leaves, flashlights flicking across every holler. By morning, there was still nothing.

And that's when Elwood Blevins showed up.

Elwood looked like a man who belonged more to the land than to people. Skin the texture of dried tobacco, eyes pale as smoke, a beard that tangled with the buttons of his shirt. He'd been a shadow in Redemption Falls for as long as anyone could remember, living in a sagging cabin up near Bear Rock Ridge, speaking only when silence had finished its say.

He waited outside the church while Jim locked up after a restless morning service. Didn't speak. Just stood there, chewing the stem of a pipe that hadn't been lit in years.

"I know where the boy is," Elwood said, finally. "But you won't find him 'less the land lets him go."

Jim had paused, keys in hand. "The sheriff's still looking."

Elwood nodded once. "He won't find nothin'."

There was no drama in his tone, no mysticism. Just certainty. The kind of certainty that doesn't ask permission.

"You came to tell me that?" Jim asked, arms crossed.

"I came to tell you how to get him back."

That night, Jim followed Elwood deep into the woods behind the church... far past the paths he knew, past the old baptizing holler, past the split-log fence no one tended anymore. The air changed out there. Got thicker. Like syrup in the lungs.

Elwood led him to a clearing where the trees grew in a perfect circle, bark stripped bare on the inside, as if something had eaten the memory off them.

At the center stood a stone, waist-high, flat and dark with lichen.

"This where they did it," Elwood said, squatting beside it. "Back when the watchers still listened. When the old families paid the price and didn't pretend the land was clean."

Jim tried to speak, but his throat had closed.

Elwood unrolled a bundle of cloth and laid it on the stone...inside were seven silver nails, a strip of bark covered in symbols, a wax-stained candle stub, and a page torn from something older than paper.

"I need your voice, preacher," Elwood muttered. "Your line's been clean. That matters."

Jim shook his head. "This isn't scripture."

"No," Elwood said. "It's older."

And Jim...trembling, uncertain...opened his mouth and began to read.

The language scratched like thorns against his tongue. Each word felt like it didn't want to be spoken aloud. The air thickened, the trees leaned in. The sky darkened... no clouds, just a draining of light.

When the ritual ended, Elwood slit a chicken's throat over the stone. The blood ran into the cracks and vanished like it had never touched the rock.

Then the wind stopped.

And a voice...not theirs... whispered through the clearing... "The debt is not forgotten."

The next morning, Eli Candler was found on the church steps, curled up and asleep, covered in leaves and mud but unharmed. Couldn't remember anything. Said he'd followed a dog into the woods, then the trees changed.

Everyone rejoiced. Everyone said God had answered.

But later that day, Sarah Pratt, the school librarian, was found dead in her home. Massive heart failure. No history of illness. She was thirty-nine.

And no one questioned it. They just...let it lie.

But Jim didn't.

He carried it.

Still does.

___Present Day

The photograph trembled in his hands. It was grainy, water damaged. He'd kept it tucked between the pages of a hymnal all these years. In it: Jim, Elwood, and a third figure...barely visible...standing by the stone. Over-exposed. Warped by time. But the symbols carved into the bark behind them were unmistakable.

The same ones Donna had asked about days ago, when she came in with that look in her eye.

The same ones he'd seen in his father's notebook, now buried in the locked drawer of the church office desk.

Jim set the photo down and opened that drawer slowly. Inside, wrapped in a black ribbon, was a single page…brittle, inked with angular writing. Not English. Not Latin. Not even Appalachian root-talk.

Alīesung.

He stared at the page for a long time.

Then, reverently, he lit a candle and began to pray.

Not to God.

But to whatever might still be listening.

Chapter 18

Ash in the Basin

The sanctuary was empty except for the faint smell of beeswax and mildew. Afternoon light spilled through the stained glass, painting bruised rainbows on the wooden pews. Donna stood just inside the open door, clutching Alīesung to her chest, uncertain whether to step forward or run back out into the sunlight.

She didn't call for him.

She didn't need to.

Pastor Jim Crowder emerged from his office like a man who had been waiting on her shadow. His gait was steady, but his eyes, blue-tinged gray like frost on tin, held a haunted flicker. His collar was unbuttoned, sleeves rolled to the forearms. He looked tired in a way that went beyond sleep.

"You're back," he said softly, not as greeting but observation.

Donna nodded, stepping into the stillness. "I read something... something I don't understand, but I think you do."

He gestured toward the front pew, then eased himself down beside her, leaving just enough space for the ghosts to breathe between them.

For a moment, the silence felt ceremonial. Then Donna placed the book beside her on the polished wood. Its cracked leather cover looked obscene next to the hymnals.

Pastor Jim stared at it but didn't reach for it.

"I was six," he said, voice low, as if speaking might rouse something in the rafters. "First time I saw it."

Donna didn't move. "Saw what?"

He hesitated. Then… "The thing that lives under the baptistry."

Her pulse quickened, but she kept still.

"Back then, this church wasn't air-conditioned. Summers were hot. My father… he was pastor then… used to leave the sanctuary open at night. Said God's breath should pass through freely." Jim chuckled without humor. "I came here once after dark. Slipped out the parsonage window. Had a flashlight. I wanted to practice my scripture reading where no one could hear me stumble."

He ran a hand over his jaw.

"I heard water," he continued. "But the basin was empty. I crept toward the front, and when I passed by the pulpit, I saw something crouched in the baptismal basin. Not a man. Not an animal. Something… shaped like a prayer you forget halfway through. Long limbs. No eyes.

Pale as candlewax, dripping with water that didn't come from any pipe."

Donna's breath caught.

"It was lapping from the basin like a thirsty dog," he whispered. "And when it noticed me, it didn't lunge. It didn't growl. It just... smiled."

Donna felt her skin tighten, gooseflesh prickling down her arms.

"My father said it was just a dream. A child's fevered imagination. But he stopped leaving the doors open at night."

He leaned back in the pew, staring up at the vaulted ceiling.

"I never told anyone else. Not my wife. Not the congregation. Not even myself, not really. I buried it beneath years of sermons and the smell of lemon polish and potlucks."

"And now?" Donna asked.

Pastor Jim's gaze dropped back to the book.

"Now I see cracks," he said. "In the floorboards. In the people. In the mirror. I used to believe this town was blessed. But it's not. It's watched. And the watchers... they've been fed before."

Donna felt something hollow open inside her. "Fed?"

"Sin," Jim murmured. "Guilt. Secrets too heavy for one soul to carry. We pass it down like inheritance. Like communion."

He turned toward her fully now, and the mask of certainty slid away from his face like old plaster.

"I see you carrying it too," he said, voice hoarse. "Same look my father wore before his hands started shaking. Same look I saw in the mirror the day after I baptized a girl who screamed when the water touched her."

Donna reached for Alīesung but stopped halfway. "You believe it," she said. "All of it."

"I do," he admitted. "And I hate myself for it."

Silence again. Thick, holy, haunted.

Then Donna said: "Something's coming, Jim. I don't know what. But it's waking up."

He nodded slowly. "I know."

They sat there until the sun dipped below the windows and the colors faded from the floor. When they finally rose, Donna reached down slowly and pick up the book. The weight has seemed to increase since she first laid it down. She held it tightly to her chest, turned and walked out... neither she nor Pastor Jim looked back.

Chapter 19

The Circle on Route 33

Beau didn't remember making the turn.

One minute, he was driving north on the old county road with nothing on his mind but coffee and asphalt...and the next, his hands were tightening around the wheel as his SUV idled at the mouth of a gravel path veiled in fog. The turnoff had no sign. Just twin tire ruts vanishing into a knot of trees.

The dashboard clock blinked 4:42 a.m.

He killed the engine.

The world outside was unnaturally still. No insects, no wind. Even the leaves seemed to hang motionless, like they were listening.

Beau climbed out, boots crunching soft gravel, the weight of his old sidearm heavy under his coat. He didn't know why he'd brought it. He never wore it unless he was working. And he wasn't supposed to be working now.

He crept forward along the path, alert to every shadow, brushing aside dew-drenched branches. The deeper he went, the less sure he became of where the path had led him.

Then he saw it.

The clearing.

Rough stones, arranged in a wide circle, barely visible under the leaf litter. No moss grew on them. No grass either. Just bare dirt, black and still as ash.

Beau stopped at the edge, his boots just touching the outer ring. His breath caught in his chest.

He'd seen this before.

Not here.

Kandahar, 2010.

His team had gone dark for 48 hours. When they finally found what was left, the gear was laid out in perfect order; helmets stacked, rifles lined up, boots side by side. But no bodies. Just a circle of scorched dirt. Same size. Same formation.

Same absence.

He hadn't told anyone then. Not what he really saw. Just followed protocol. Filed a report. Pushed it down with the rest of it.

But now, standing in the woods of Tennessee, that old dread curled up the back of his spine.

He crouched by the nearest stone.

Symbols had been scratched into the face of it... barely visible through the grime. Not English. Not Arabic. Not any alphabet he knew. But the angles, the slashes, the curling spirals...

They matched what he'd seen before. He'd heard about these kinds of things. Beau had grown up in a place just like Redemption Falls and the Appalachian lore was thick with old world sigils.

Beau exhaled slowly.

At the center of the circle sat a low mound of ash. Beneath it...he brushed it aside...was a burned candle stub. And hair. Human hair, bound in red thread, half-melted into the wax.

He stood up too fast.

The forest groaned.

Not wind.

A sound older than wind. Like trees shifting in their roots. Or something beneath the dirt turning over in its sleep.

Then he heard it

"It's not time yet."

A whisper. A child's voice. Directly behind him.

Beau spun.

Nothing.

Just trees. Shadows. And the brittle silence of a place that had waited too long to be seen.

He backed out of the clearing without turning his back.

Didn't run. Didn't speak.

He walked with purpose, hands clenched, eyes on the trail.

Back in his SUV, he slammed the door shut and jammed the key into the ignition. The engine turned over reluctantly, like it too, wanted to stay.

He didn't look in the rearview mirror until he hit pavement again. When he did, the woods behind him looked darker than before. Like something had stepped out of the circle...and wasn't finished watching.

Chapter 20

Dan's Doubt

The Galveston airport was all glass and humidity, and Dan Miller felt like a ghost moving through it. He adjusted the strap of his laptop bag and ignored the buzz of incoming emails on his phone. Another client. Another coastal remediation briefing. Another half-week spent in a hotel room trying not to wonder if his wife was slipping away from him.

That night, alone in his hotel suite, Dan opened the shared cloud folder they kept for bills and kids' paperwork.

A mundane ritual, something to tether him to their life. But a new folder caught his eye:

PRIVATE_DO NOT OPEN

Dan blinked. Donna never labeled things like that. She barely remembered to tag documents, let alone encrypt them.

He opened it.

Inside: fragments. Scans of notebook pages in Donna's handwriting. A few audio clips.

He clicked on the first text file.

"I think I'm losing time again. Last night I lit a candle, and when I opened my eyes, it was daylight. My hands smelled like wax and iron. I think something spoke to me, but the voice was mine."

He scrolled.

"There are markings on the baseboards. I didn't make them. I've tried cleaning them off. They come back."

He called her.

Straight to voicemail.

He waited fifteen minutes, pacing his hotel room.

Then he tried again.

Still nothing.

The next morning, he checked her location.

Still in Redemption Falls.

Still moving around town.

Still alive, he guessed.

He texted her:

"Hey. Just checking in. You okay?"

A minute passed.

Then three.

Still no reply.

By midweek, Donna hadn't returned his calls. Her texts had grown sparse. Short phrases. One just read: "Don't speak your full name aloud." Another: "The salt didn't hold last night."

Dan sat in a sterile conference room, pretending to take notes while wondering what the hell that meant. Dan opened a blank email draft. He addressed it to her but didn't send it. He just stared at the blinking cursor.

Subject: What's happening?

He typed nothing else.

Closed his laptop.

Sat in the dark.

Outside, the Gulf storm was beginning to press against the windows, gentle and growing. Thunder murmured somewhere deep in the sky. The same kind of storm he used to love.

Now it felt like a mirror of something else.

He didn't sleep.

Back home, he imagined their house quiet. Too quiet.

He imagined the smell of burned wax. The flicker of candlelight at the edge of vision.

And he realized the worst part wasn't that he couldn't reach Donna.

It was that something else might already have.

Chapter 21

A Promise to Keep

Beau Carter pushed open the screen door of Momma's on Main Street, the hinges letting out a familiar whine before snapping shut on an autumn breeze. He stepped inside, nodding toward the counter, where Luanne was topping off someone's coffee with her usual smile.

She looked up and grinned. "Well, look who's back."

Beau returned the smile, faint but genuine. "Didn't figure I'd find a better breakfast this side of the mountains."

Luanne flipped her order pad shut with a satisfied snap. "You planning on staying a while, or just another fly-by?"

Beau glanced toward the window, where fall leaves danced along the sidewalk like rust-colored secrets. He exhaled slowly. "Looks like for a while, anyway."

"Good," she said, already turning back toward the coffee pot. "Town could use a few more steady souls."

He made his way to a booth tucked along the far wall, slid into the vinyl seat, and wrapped his hands around the mug Luanne brought over without needing to ask. The heat seeped into his fingers. Outside, the wind wound itself through the branches like a sermon looking for a congregation.

A few minutes passed, quiet except for the low hum of conversation and the hiss of bacon on the griddle.

Then the door creaked again.

Donna stepped inside. Her cheeks were pink from the cold, her dark hair wind-tossed. She hesitated a moment in the doorway...book-laden tote slung over one shoulder… her gaze sweeping the room like a wary animal entering unfamiliar woods. There was something haunted in the set of her jaw, something that said she hadn't slept well in days.

She spotted the open booth.

He was there.

The man from the ridge.

Broad shoulders. That same weather-worn look. A protective stillness, like a wall that didn't ask questions but wouldn't let you fall. His eyes lifted and caught hers...gray, steady, and a little wounded. She didn't hesitate. She walked toward him like the only safe place in the room.

She slid into the seat across from him.

Beau gave a small nod. Not a greeting...an understanding.

Before either could speak, Luanne arrived, notepad in hand and a sly, knowing gleam in her eye.

"Well, look at this," she teased. "You two know each other?"

Donna blinked. "Oh...I... no. I didn't mean to intrude, I just..."

Beau interrupted gently, "Don't mind. Company's company. Long as you don't talk politics or religion before I finish this bacon."

Luanne chuckled. "You're in good hands, sweetheart. He says that to everybody."

As she disappeared toward the kitchen, the quiet settled back in...not the brittle awkwardness of strangers with nothing to say, but something denser, humming just beneath the surface. It was the kind of silence that carried weight. Tension, yes, but not the sharp-edged kind. This felt more like recognition. Like standing in a place you'd never been but somehow knew. Something half-remembered, waiting on the tongue for a name.

"You local?" Beau asked eventually, his voice casual, but tuned in like a man listening for the turn of a key in an old lock.

Donna came back with her mug and a nod. She sat slowly, wrapping both hands around the warm ceramic like it might anchor her. "Born and raised," she said. "Donna Miller. Used to go by Ogle."

Beau's brow lifted, something flickering in his eyes…not quite surprise, more like a page turning in his mind. "Ogle, huh. I served with a Tommy Ogle once. Quiet guy. Smart as hell. Deadeye shot."

The air shifted. Donna stopped breathing for a moment.

"Tommy Ogle?" she echoed, almost a whisper. "My brother's name was Tommy. He… he died overseas. We never got much…just that he'd been killed in action. No real story, no one who saw it happen. Just… silence."

Beau straightened, not sharply but as if shedding something…his guarded posture, the easy lean. His whole presence shifted, like a man stepping out from behind a shadow.

"Was your brother tall?" he asked gently. "Sandy blonde hair? Had a way of laughing at things nobody else found funny?"

Donna's eyes glistened. "Yeah... that's him. That's Tommy."

"It was Kandahar," Beau said quietly. "2010. We were in the same fire team. He saved my ass more than once. Hell, more than I deserved. Called me 'Boots,' even after I made rank. Said I stomped around like a man born in thunder."

A soft, broken laugh escaped her. "That sounds like him."

They looked at each other across the table...two people not quite strangers, not quite family, but suddenly tethered by something unspoken and old.

"I didn't think I'd ever meet someone who knew him like that," Donna said, voice thick.

"I still hear him sometimes," Beau replied. "Singing Springsteen under his breath when things got bad. Always the same line...'tramps like us, baby we were born to run.' Said it helped drown out the rest of it."

Her throat caught. Before she could think twice, her hand reached across the table and found his. It wasn't rehearsed or careful. Just instinct. Her fingers trembled slightly, and she hated that, but Beau didn't let go. He held her hand like someone who knew the value of a grip in the dark.

They sat like that in the hush. The refrigerator clicked to life, the wind curled itself around the eaves, and for once, she didn't brace against the silence. She let it fill her instead. Something in her…something that had been clenched for years…began to loosen.

After a long moment, Beau spoke again. His voice was quieter now, almost reverent. "Tommy used to talk about home like it was a story he couldn't finish. Said it held more ghosts than graves. I never knew what he meant."

Donna swallowed hard. "He wasn't wrong."

Beau didn't push. He just watched her…steady, present. Like he knew not to ask too much too fast. Like he'd been on the edge of hard things before and understood what it meant to wait.

And for the first time in a long while, Donna didn't feel quite so alone in the remembering.

Donna broke the silence. "I found something… something that shouldn't exist. A very old book."

"Ok?" Beau replied waiting for the important bit of information that should be coming.

"Yea, it's…it's got something to do with my past… actually the history of Redemption Falls and most likely further back than that." Donna explained.

"Look, I'm headed to see a friend down at The Book Nook, it's where I found this book, you wanna come along? My friend, Jess, has known Tommy and I since we were little…maybe you could learn a little more about him and where we come from, and I could learn a little more about this book."

"The Book Nook huh?" Beau replied…uncertain.
"Sure, it'd be great to meet any friend of Tommy's."

Chapter 22

Cracked Glass

The bell above the door gave a hollow jangle as Donna stepped into the Book Nook, Beau... close behind. Morning sun slanted through the blinds, striping the floor in golden bars, but something was off. The quiet was too quiet. No Ella Fitzgerald. No French press coffee scent. No Jess humming tunelessly from the back.

Then she saw it the front case's glass cracked clean through. A little bloom of shattered safety glass glittered on the carpet beneath it.

"Jess?" Donna called.

From behind the counter, Jess emerged, a hand on her hip and a tightness around her eyes Donna didn't like.

"You're early," Jess said. "I was going to call you in a bit."

"What happened?" Beau asked, scanning the shop with a soldier's precision.

Jess motioned toward the damage. "Break-in. Last night. Nothin's missing. Some mess in the back room. No real sign of forced entry, but the lock on the back door's jimmied."

"Cops?" Donna asked.

Jess shook her head. "What would they do? I filed a report, sure. But they just shrugged. Said it was probably kids or a drifter looking for cash. But I..." she hesitated, then looked directly at Donna. "I already know it was Sam."

Donna blinked. "Sam Hayes?"

Jess nodded slowly. "He came in yesterday morning, maybe ten minutes after you left. Said he was looking for something specific. Kept glancing around like someone was listening. Then asked if I had a book here...a book bound in hide and very old."

Beau shifted beside her. "He asked about the book?"

"Obsessed," Jess said. "Wouldn't even name it. Just kept saying, 'The old one. The one with the symbols.' I told him it was gone, but he didn't believe me. Got real agitated and ran out. Creeped me out, honestly."

Donna's heart pounded like a fist on a locked door.

Beau's voice was steady, too steady. "What's in that book, Donna?"

She didn't answer right away. Her eyes scanned the edges of the store, half-expecting something to rise from the shadows. Then she looked at Jess, whose face was carved with worry, and at Beau, who stood like he was ready to take a bullet that hadn't been fired yet.

"I didn't mean to get you involved," she said softly.

Beau stepped closer. "You didn't. I walked in on my own. Now tell me...what's going on?"

Donna reached into her bag and pulled out the book. Even wrapped in an old tea towel, it felt warm in her hands. Alive.

"It's not just a book. It's...called Aliesung. Or at least that's what's written on the title page. I found it in a box of old books here at The Book Nook yesterday. It wasn't cataloged. I don't think it was supposed to be here."

Beau took it, carefully unwrapping it just enough to see the cover. The binding was cracked but intact, and the lettering along the spine was hand-inked and slightly slanted, like a private language.

Jess leaned in but didn't touch it. "That's the book I sold you yesterday...and that's what he was looking for?"

"I think so," Donna said. "But it's not just the book. I read from it."

Beau's head turned sharply. "Read from it? Like an incantation or somethin'?"

She nodded. "There's a rite...an invocation, maybe. I did it. Alone. Outside on my back patio."

Beau swore under his breath.

Jess took a half-step back. "Donna..."

"I didn't know what I was doing," she said quickly. "I just felt...called. And afterward, things started happening. I remembered things I hadn't thought of in years. Dreams that followed me into waking. Faces I shouldn't know."

"And Sam?" Beau asked. "How's he tied to this?"

"Sam's my ex-husband and we have been in a conflict over custody of my two sons. I... I don't know exactly how he's tied to Aliesung, but I do know that his family name keeps coming up in its writings again and again. But I think he's looking for something the book might unlock. Gaining power would definitely be a motivation for him."

Beau was quiet for a long beat, processing.

Then he said, "Where do we go from here?"

Donna hesitated...but only for a breath. "There's someone who might know more. Betty Lou Tipton. She knows about the old rites. My grandmother used to talk about her before people in Redemption Falls started forgetting."

"Cable's Holler," Jess murmured.

Beau nodded. "Then we go to Cable's Holler."

Jess didn't follow right away. Her gaze lingered on the mess near the occult shelf, then back to the front case, as if the weight of what had happened was only now settling over her. Slowly, she walked around the counter and knelt beside the shattered bloom of glass.

"I almost forgot," she said, brushing aside a few scattered pamphlets and dust-jacket fragments. "After he ran...after the books fell...something slipped out."

She straightened, holding a weathered envelope between two fingers.

"I read it...sorry, I couldn't help myself when I saw it made out to you." Jess winced a little as she spoke.

"That's ok... a letter?" Donna asked.

"Yea...from your granny Ada."

It was thin, the paper yellowed, the edges soft from age. On the front, in an elegant, looping hand, was written:

To my Donna - when you begin to remember.

--Granny Ada

Jess handed it to her without another word.

Donna took it carefully, as though the paper might crumble in her hands. Her breath caught in her throat. She hadn't seen that handwriting in decades... not since the funeral. Her fingers trembled as she unfolded the single page inside.

The ink was faded but legible, as though Granny Ada had written it in firelight and sorrow.

"Child,

If this letter finds you, then what I feared has begun to stir. You may not recall the old rites, nor the price paid in blood and silence, but they are stitched into your marrow. The sin eaters kept balance...not just of soul, but of all that lies beneath. When one forgets, the veil begins to fray. When all forget...well. The hunger beneath remembers.

This world isn't built to hold back what we buried. And if it rises, it won't come as flame or flood. It'll come as shadow that knows your name.

Forgive me, Donna. I prayed you'd never have to know. But I see now...I was only ever delaying the storm.

When it comes, you'll have to choose. Be the last of us...Or be the first."

Donna's lips moved soundlessly as she read the last line again, and again.

Jess stepped closer. "I thought it was just another note tucked in a book. But then I saw your name."

Beau said nothing, watching her carefully.

Donna folded the letter back along its creases like it was a part of her, old and essential. She looked up, eyes glossy but clear.

"I think," she said, "this is bigger than any of us thought."

And outside, as if in answer, the wind stirred through the alley's narrow mouth. Not loud...but enough to make the bell above the door jingle once more, soft and final.

Donna and Beau left the store together, the letter tucked into Donna's coat pocket, the book cradled like a relic between Beau's hands.

Cable's Holler was waiting.

And something else was waking.

Chapter 23

Betty Lou

Beau's SUV groaned as it crawled up the backwoods track into Cable's Holler, its tires spinning wildly before latching onto loose gravel. Rocks clattered and pinged against the undercarriage, the incline growing steeper, less forgiving. The gravel thinned, gave way to naked earth and jagged stone, forcing the engine into a deep growl. The vehicle bucked and twisted like a mule, and Beau fought the wheel, his arms yanking left and right with each sudden lurch of the climb.

"So, this lady..." he muttered, squinting through the windshield at the snaking road ahead.

"Betty Lou," Donna said, her voice taut as she clung to the overhead handle, her knuckles pale against the plastic.

"Right. Betty Lou... she knows something? About the book?"

Donna turned her head sharply, her ponytail swinging with the motion. The SUV jolted over a root, throwing her against the seatbelt. She didn't answer at first, eyes fixed on Beau.

"If anyone does," she finally said, "it's her."

Up the hill, a screen door creaked open on rusted hinges.

Betty Lou Tipton stepped onto her porch broom-first, swatting a cobweb from the eave before setting to her morning routine. Dust lifted in lazy swirls as she brushed the boards clean, pausing now and then to glance at the sky like it might offer a hint about the day ahead.

The old hen coop waited. So did the egg basket, the feed pail, and the cow that lowed impatiently beyond the fence line. Every step of the morning belonged to her; the rhythm carved over eighty-five years on this same mountain ridge. Her world wasn't big...but it was hers. She'd never seen the ocean, never walked the streets of a city. Didn't need to. The holler had offered enough mystery, enough joy and pain and lessons to fill a dozen lifetimes.

Her broom paused mid-sweep.

Far below, tires crunched over stone and clay...an unfamiliar sound, rising from the slope like a question.

She narrowed her eyes, creases folding deep into weathered skin. Visitors didn't stumble up her hill by accident. If someone came knocking, it meant something. Always did.

The SUV finally rolled to a stop in a cloud of dust and engine heat. Beau cut the ignition, but the vehicle still ticked with protest. Donna was already out, boots crunching on the rocky earth as she took in the small homestead...a weathered cabin crouched beneath a canopy of oak, smoke curling faintly from a bent stovepipe.

Betty Lou didn't move from the porch. She leaned on her broom like a staff, eyes locked on the two strangers who now stepped toward her with a kind of cautious reverence. She wore a faded house dress and scuffed boots, her silver hair braided into a rope down her back. Her presence, even in stillness, carried weight.

Donna raised a hand in greeting, her voice softer than usual. "Ms. Tipton?"

Betty Lou didn't answer right away. She squinted at Donna like she was peering through fog...or trying to place her in a dream from long ago.

"You're Barbara Jean's girl," she said at last, not a question but a quiet, certain truth. "Ain't seen you since you was knee-high and hollerin'."

Donna nodded. "That's me. This is my friend, Beau."

Betty Lou gave Beau a polite nod, but her eyes drifted back to Donna, narrowing just a little. "Didn't recognize you at first. You favor your mama, but there's a piece of Ada in you too. Especially 'round the eyes."

Donna's breath caught for half a second. "You knew my grandmother?"

"Child," Betty Lou said, her voice dipping low, "everyone knew your grandmother. Not the way folks know their neighbors...not wave-from-the-porch knowin'. I mean knew her. In their bones. In the back of their minds when the night got too quiet."

Donna glanced at Beau, unsure whether to smile or flinch. "She...she was a midwife, right?"

Betty Lou gave a dry chuckle. "That's what they said. She did more'n that, though. Folks didn't call her a witch...least not where she could hear...but they came knockin' when the doctor's remedies failed, or the preacher stopped answerin' the door. Charms for fevers. Salves for spirits. Rites for things too heavy to speak plain."

She paused, then leaned forward, voice softer now, like the words weren't meant to travel far.

"Ada knew the old ways. Appalachian ways. Things passed down in hushes and sideways looks...moonlight rites, salt lines on windowsills, bowls of milk left out for what couldn't be buried proper. Some say she took on sins when no priest would come. Others say she saw things before they happened and just didn't always speak on 'em."

Donna felt her mouth go dry. "I don't remember much."

"You were just a little thing," Betty Lou said, kindly now. "But I 'member once...you sittin' by the window while she whispered over a bowl of milk. Said it was for a baby that never got held."

"I thought I dreamed that," Donna murmured.

"No, baby. You didn't. You were marked by it. All them years you spent tryin' to be like the rest of us...college, shakin' off the dust...you still carried it. Some things don't wash out."

Donna looked down at her hands. They trembled.

"She was a wise woman," Betty Lou went on. "When folks weren't callin' her cursed."

The silence between them stretched, filled only by the rustling of wind through dry leaves.

Betty Lou folded her arms and gave Donna a look...not unkind, but unblinking. "You didn't just come here for a visit, did you?"

Betty Lou's eyes shifted to Beau...quick, sharp, measuring. She didn't offer a smile.

"We came because we've got questions," Donna continued. "About a book."

Betty Lou took a half step toward Donna...tilting her head to the left in a manner that communicated that she suspected she already knew the answer to the question she about to ask... "What book would that be dear?"

Donna winced and tightened her shoulders as she said the name "Alīesung."

The word seemed to pull something taut in the old woman's posture. She didn't flinch, didn't blink. But her grip on the broom tightened just enough for the wood to creak beneath her hand.

"I ain't seen it," she said flatly, then added, "and I ain't looking to."

Beau stepped forward, polite but persistent. "You've heard of it, though?"

Betty Lou exhaled through her nose, slow. She leaned the broom against the porch rail and stepped down onto the dirt, her boots thudding with a finality that made the birds in the trees fall silent.

"I've heard more than I wanted to," she said. "Enough to know that book's got a shadow on it. Folks who come sniffin' after it tend to end up different... or don't end up at all."

Donna frowned. "What do you mean?"

Betty Lou looked past them for a moment, eyes scanning the ridgeline like she half-expected something to be watching from the trees.

"What I mean is that people like Ezra Hayes thought it was something to be controlled, and he and his family took on sorrow for it....and that's all I'll say."

Beau felt a chill settle across his shoulders.

"You're saying it's cursed?"

"I'm sayin' it's dangerous," Betty Lou replied, voice dropping to a whisper like she was afraid the hills might overhear. "And it don't care what damage it leaves behind."

The porch groaned as she turned back toward her cabin. "If you know what's good for ya, you'll turn that fancy car around and forget you ever heard of that book."

She didn't wait for a reply. The screen door slapped shut behind her.

Donna didn't speak. Her head dipped, eyes fixed on the brittle leaves scattered across the ground, though she didn't seem to see them. Her shoulders sagged, as if something had settled there...heavy and sudden. A slow breath escaped her lips, more sigh than exhale.

She turned toward Beau's SUV, not all at once, but like someone caught between two worlds. One foot moved, then the other, each step careful, unsure. Her hand brushed the edge of her coat as if to steady herself.

Behind her, Betty Lou's words still hung in the air like smoke, curling around the pieces of memory and ritual Donna's mind had buried. The taste of ash clung to the back of her throat. And as she walked, the weight of the book...the rite...settled into place, no longer just strange, but dangerous. The bumpy ride along the mountain road seemed to open Donna's mind as to what she had thought was a dream...now becoming a fully developed memory. The little things began to trickle into view...it was the wind that came back to her memory first...

The wind always sounded different up on her Granny Ada's ridge. It whispered low through the pines, like someone muttering just beyond the windowpane. Not angry, not kind. Just present. Watching. Listening.

She was five, maybe six. Small enough to curl on the braided rug beneath the front window without being noticed. Her mother, Barbara Jean, had driven down the mountain that morning to stock up on a few things, and Donna had begged to stay behind. Ada had agreed, in her usual quiet way, with a glance and the tiniest nod. That was how Ada answered most things… with a look that said she already knew what would happen and had simply decided not to interfere.

The house smelled of beeswax and pine sap. Warm wood and old linen. Outside, crows fussed in the bare branches. Inside, the fire ticked softly in the stone hearth, and Ada moved like a shadow, slow and certain.

Donna watched her grandmother from the corner of one eye, pretending to be asleep.

Ada stood at the old hutch, pouring milk… real milk, still thick and warm from Miss Lila's morning cow, into a small, chipped bowl. She carried it in both hands like it was something sacred, then set it gently on the windowsill where the sun hit the wood floor in a crooked beam.

She didn't speak at first. Just stood there, one hand hovering over the bowl, the other fumbling in her apron pocket. She pulled out a small bundle wrapped in muslin, untied it, and sprinkled something into the milk…dried petals, maybe. Or herbs. Something sharp-smelling and blue-gray. It made Donna's nose itch even from across the room.

Then Ada began to whisper.

Her voice wasn't loud, but it was steady… rhythmic, like wind through tall grass or the hush of water over stones. The words weren't English. Not exactly. Some syllables curled strange and soft, like the hush-hush sounds

Donna's mama made when she thought she was out of earshot and needed to cry.

The whispering went on for several minutes. Ada's eyes stayed closed, her hand still over the bowl. Donna held her breath, afraid even blinking would break whatever spell her grandmother was weaving.

Then, without looking down, Ada said, "You can come out now, child."

Donna froze.

Ada turned her head just slightly, not startled, not angry… just calm, like she'd been expecting her the whole time. "Ain't polite to spy. But I don't mind. Better you see than go wondering."

Donna pushed herself up slowly and crossed the room, toes silent on the rug. She stood beside her grandmother, barely tall enough to see over the windowsill. The bowl of milk shimmered in the sunlight, tiny flecks of green and gray swirling slowly on its surface.

"What's it for?" she asked, her voice small.

Ada didn't answer right away. She looked down at Donna, her eyes pale and deep, like river stone. "It's for a child who didn't get to be held."

Donna frowned. "Like a ghost?"

Ada's mouth twitched at one corner. "Not quite. Ghosts want to be seen. This one just wants to rest."

"Did you know them?"

"I knew the mama. She lived just over the ridge, where the apple trees lean. Lost the baby in winter. No preacher would come. So, I do what I can."

Donna stared at the bowl. It looked so simple. Just milk and leaves and light. But it felt like more. Like it was holding something heavy and invisible.

"Will the baby see it?"

"I think so. Not with eyes like ours. But in the way birds find warm air and dogs know when it's gonna rain."

Donna leaned closer. "What if they're still sad?"

Ada's hand came down gently on her shoulder. "That's why we leave the milk. Not to fix the sadness. Just to sit with it a while."

For a long moment, neither of them spoke. The wind moved through the trees again, and this time Donna thought she heard a hum in it. Not a voice. Not exactly. But something like music made of memory.

"Can I leave a bowl too someday?" she asked.

Ada looked at her for a long time, something unreadable in her gaze. Then she nodded, once. "You already know how. Your heart remembers."

Donna didn't know what that meant, not then. But years later, she would.

That night, Donna dreamt of a baby wrapped in smoke, floating just beyond the edge of the woods. Its face was soft and turned away. It didn't cry. It didn't speak. But when it passed her, she felt something lift from her chest… a sadness that wasn't hers but had nested there anyway.

She never told her mother.

_____An abrupt jolt brought Donna's focus back to the bumpy mountain road, inside Beau's SUV and as her gaze traveled up the ridge something grabbed her attention like long fingernails into the skin of an apple..." Stop!" she shouted.

Beau's shoulders tightened...face grimaced as he slammed on the breaks, gripping the steering wheel tighter, the sound of rocks flicking on the underside of the SUV and a plume of mountain dust now migrated across the vehicle.

"What is it?!" Beau asked, still a little tense.

"That ridge...I think I know it..." Donna looked back at Beau, her eyes wide like saucers with an unspoken request...

"Really?" Beau asked, already knowing the answer.

The forest grew darker the higher they climbed...older, denser, full of a hush that wasn't quite silence. The kind of stillness that held memory. The trail narrowed into a winding cut between roots and underbrush, the laurel thickets clawing at Donna's coat. Her breath came in little white puffs.

In her bag, Aliesung shifted with each step, as if it had weight beyond the physical.

"You sure this is the place?" Beau asked, stepping over a gnarled root. "Feels like we crossed out of the world about ten minutes ago. GPS went out a ways back."

Donna didn't answer right away. She stopped beside a broad, lichen-covered stone and opened the book. The page she'd marked had grown soft with humidity, but the old handwriting remained:

"Where the ridge splits stone like broken teeth,

the watchers stir beneath."

"I recognize this," she said softly. "My grandmother brought me here when I was little. Once.

She didn't speak much about it. Called it 'the high place.' I thought it was just a dream. Until I saw this." She touched the page. "Tooth Ridge."

Beau cast a glance around. "Sounds like the start of a story where people go missing."

They crested the slope and stepped into a clearing… a bare granite shelf nestled into the mountain. All around the edge stood small cairns… neat stacks of stone, some tied with red string or wrapped with dried herb bundles. Symbols had been etched into some of the stones, faint now with time.

The trees around the clearing bowed away, as though they didn't want to see what went on here.

Donna took a slow breath. "This is older than anything I was told. Older than the Ogle family. They didn't perform the rites. But they remembered. They were asked to watch, to carry the memory without speaking it aloud."

Beau was quiet, taking in the space like a man reading a language he didn't know.

And then, from the edge of the clearing, a voice rasped…

"Ogle blood was meant to watch and carry."

A woman stepped from the trees…wrapped in layers of faded cloth, hair twisted and pinned with bits of bone and copper. Her cane clicked softly against stone as she walked. One of her eyes was clouded, but the other fixed sharply on Donna.

"You carry the book," the woman said. "That's dangerous, even unopened."

Beau stepped closer to Donna, hand hovering near instinct.

"I'm not here to cause harm," Donna said. "I'm trying to understand."

The woman came forward, her gaze still pinned to the book.

"My name is Mavis Williams," she said. "I am the last of the four who were taught the words...not to perform them, but to remember what they meant. And what they cost."

Donna's breath caught. "My grandmother...Ada Ogle...she brought me here once. I think she knew you."

Mavis gave a single nod. "She did. Ada bore witness. She wasn't one of us, but she understood the weight of memory. The Ogle women were like carved bowls...we poured the story into them so it wouldn't be lost."

Donna stepped forward; book still tucked in her arms. "This book...Aliesung...I found it in a bookstore. The writing is a combination of old languages that I haven't seen before as well as English. The parts I can read... don't read like folklore. The read like family history and instructions."

"That's because it is," Mavis said. "But not just instruction. Obligation. Most folk think sin-eating was just ceremony...bread on the chest, salt by the mouth. They never ask what came after. Never ask what happened to the ones who carried that weight too long."

She gestured to the cairns, memorial mounds made of bone and stone. "This place is where the last rites were done. Not just for the dead, but for the eaters themselves. When their bodies broke under the burden. When their minds stopped being their own."

Donna's voice was small. "Why would anyone choose that?"

"They didn't always choose," Mavis said. "Some were born marked. Some were taken young and taught to hold silence like breath. Most didn't live long. And those who did... weren't right when they did."

Beau frowned. "And this book? It teaches all that?"

Mavis looked to Donna; her expression almost tender. "Aliesung is not just about the dead. It's about memory…blood memory and ancestral weight. The ways pain echoes forward when you try to bury it too deep."

Donna opened the book to the page again. "I read a piece of it. Just one passage. And afterward, I started remembering things I don't think I ever lived. Faces. Names. A prayer whispered under floorboards."

"That's how it begins," Mavis murmured. "The book doesn't just tell you what was done. It shows you. It pulls you down into it. If your line ever bore witness to the rites, even once, it can wake that blood."

"I need to know the rest," Donna said. "I need to understand what it means…my ex-husband, Sam Hayes, is up to something and it involves this book."

"Hayes family abused the rite and claimed it as a legacy for their own family line, but it was never really theirs to begin with." Mavis said, pinching her brow with spite.

Mavis calmed her posture and stared at her for a long time. The mountain wind moved gently between them, cool and earthy, carrying the scent of woodsmoke and dry moss.

"You need to remember first," she said. "There is another place, darker and older. One not written down. You'll need to go there; only then can the book make a vessel of you. This place will have a circle made of stones. Noting grows in the circle but darkness. That's where the rite will have to be completed… or closed."

Beau shifted beside Donna. "I've been there…I've seen this place already. Seen the circle."

Mavis turned her milky eye to him. "The circle is the key. That's where this will have to be completed."

Donna looked down at Aliesung. The symbols on the page no longer looked like ink. They looked like old blood, dried into the page, waiting.

She nodded once.

"Ok, thank you Mavis."

Mavis just nodded once then turned to walk away.

Donna and Beau started the walk back down the ridge.

Chapter 24

The Pact

Outside, the wind picked up. The skies over Redemption Falls darkened slightly, though no storm had been forecast. The light shifted...not dimming exactly but turning a shade older. As if the sun had passed through something ancient on its way to dusk.

At the far edge of the Hayes land, beyond the rust-eaten fence and the remains of a long-collapsed smoke-house, the twelve stones formed a silent ring. Time had tried to bury them, but the earth always spit them back out.

Outside the circle the grass grew uneven, curling inward, like it too understood this was a place not meant for trespass.

A crow landed at the center, its wings twitching with unease. It cawed once, hopped forward...

...and then collapsed.

Stone dead.

Its eyes turned wide and gleaming white, like pearls left in ash.

From the tree line, Sam Hayes watched, the taste of iron blooming at the back of his tongue. Not fear. Not guilt. Something older.

He pressed a hand to the thick scar beneath his shirt...the one his father gave him on the day he was "named." It burned now, the skin taut, the brand alive a-gain.

"They've found each other," he muttered. "Damn the timing."

He stepped forward, boots sinking into the soft, sour soil. The twelve stones pulsed faintly beneath his gaze, as if sensing the tension in the pact. The tether was straining.

The land stirred. Something beneath it shifted...not in form, but in intent.

Sam clenched his fists.

"She doesn't even know what she carries," he said aloud. "And he..."

"He's still half-made. Grief and regret do not make a vessel."

The wind circled once, dragging leaves around the stones in a slow spiral. Sam crouched at the edge of the ring, drawing a sigil in the dirt with the tip of a rusted nail.

"She wants to gain control of my flesh and blood...my sons. This is their birthright, if she gets help and continues to press, she could ruin everything."

He paused, looking up at the stones.

"And I won't let that happen."

The pact had been set in his bloodline. Not chosen but inherited...a burden mistaken for honor. For four generations, the Hayes had bound the gate, fed it small things...a lamb, a name, a shadow whispered through red twine. But the land was hungrier now. It wanted more. It wanted balance.

And balance meant Donna Miller.

And the man who once should've died ... Beau Carter.

Together, they completed something Sam had been carefully keeping incomplete.

He stood.

"They don't really matter," he told the stones. "I've given enough. I've bled. I've bound. The gate will open my way."

Another gust of wind peeled through the trees, rattling the bone charms that hung from the old barn door. A low groan sounded from beneath the earth. Not yet the gate...just the thing behind it, stirring in anticipation.

Sam stepped back from the circle, wiping his hands on the front of his jeans. The crow still lay in the center, white-eyed and motionless, like a sigil in its own right.

He glanced west...toward town, toward her.

Chapter 25

Down the Mountain

Beau and Donna were back in the SUV making the difficult drive back down the mountain. At first Donna said nothing, watching her own palms as though trying to read the tangled lines writhing there. The memory of Mavis's words had left her raw and unsteady, as if her mind had broken open a seam she'd never meant to touch. She could not escape the sensation that she hadn't chosen any of this, not really; she was simply the latest in a chain of women who had been taught to hold silence like breath.

They coasted onto the county highway, the washboard rattle of washout giving way to the softer, steadier hum of pavement, and the tension between them shifted, went slack.

"Thank you," said Donna at last, her voice dry and unpolished.

"For what?" asked Beau, eyes still fixed on the road ahead.

"For not...for not telling me I'm crazy. Or worse, treating me like I'm breakable." She didn't mean for the words to sound so small, but they did. She swallowed hard, as if the truth might still turn bitter in her mouth.

Beau didn't answer right away. His hands stayed steady on the wheel, fingers loose but firm, the way someone drives when they've seen too much to jerk the wheel without good reason. The trees flashed past in green and gold blurs, and the sky ahead had begun to lower, heavy with an afternoon storm not yet born.

"You're not breakable," he said finally. "You're just waking up."

Donna turned her head toward the window, blinking back the heat behind her eyes. "It doesn't feel like waking up. It feels like drowning."

"Yeah," Beau said, almost to himself. "Sometimes it's both."

They passed a faded barn with a rusted roof, and for a long moment, the silence came back, not tense now, but tired… bone-deep tired, the kind that settles in when the weight you've been carrying finally shifts but doesn't leave.

Donna let her head rest against the window, the coolness of the glass grounding her. "Do you think any of it matters? All that Mavis said. The rites. The blood. The forgetting."

Beau exhaled through his nose, like he'd been holding something in too long. "I think it matters if you say it does. I think maybe it always mattered… but now you get to decide what that means."

A soft rumble rolled across the hills behind them, thunder still far off but promising.

Donna closed her eyes, and for the first time in a long while, she didn't try to chase the memories that stirred beneath her skin. She just let them rise, like mist from the forest floor... uncertain, shapeless, but real.

And in the hush between thunder and rain, the mountain no longer felt quite so far behind.

The Naming

The wind howled low through the ridgeline that night, curling around the old stones like it remembered every name carved into them.

Ezra Hayes stood at the outer edge of the circle, coat flapping behind him like a broken wing. His boots sank into the wet moss, and in his left hand, he gripped the leather-bound book...Alīesung...with knuckles white and blood-speckled. In the center of the circle, his son knelt bare-chested, shaking.

Samuel Joseph Hayes. Seventeen. Just a boy, but not for long.

Ezra's voice scraped the cold: "You ready to carry this name?"

Sam nodded, jaw clenched tight, fists pressed to his thighs. He didn't speak. Didn't need to. Ezra could see the fire in his eyes, same as his own father had seen in him. That ancient hunger passed down like marrow. And fear, too...that was right. It meant the boy understood what this was.

Behind him, the elders watched. Five of them. Men with hollow eyes and tobacco-stained teeth, their flannel collars buttoned tight despite the summer heat that clung like rot. They held no lanterns. The stones glowed enough on their own now. As they always did when blood was about to be spoken.

Ezra opened the book.

The air shifted.

Inside, the page bore the same words it had for generations:

To bind the gate and honor the pact, a name must be given in the shadow of the moon. Blood must speak. Flesh must kneel. The cost will follow the line.

He drew the knife from its sheath. The handle was deer antler, worn smooth. The blade was old iron, blackened by age and rites too long remembered.

Sam looked up once...just once...and Ezra saw something in his eyes that almost stopped him.

It was his mother's defiance. The kind of stubborn, steel-backed refusal that had driven her to take Sam and leave when he was still swaddled in a flannel blanket.

She'd failed.

Ezra had brought him back.

"Speak the name," one of the elders rasped.

Ezra stepped into the ring.

He held the blade to his palm and cut.

Blood welled, then fell in heavy drops onto the moss. It hissed, steam curling where it touched stone.

"I name him Samuel Joseph Hayes," Ezra said, voice rising. "Flesh of my flesh. Bound by the rite. Carrier of the tether."

The wind screamed through the trees.

Ezra reached into his coat and pulled out the offering…a chicken, its throat already slit, its feathers still warm. He laid it gently at his son's knees.

Sam flinched. Not from the bird...from the book, which pulsed in Ezra's hand like it had a heart.

Ezra turned the page.

There, scrawled in his father's hand, was the failed name:

Thomas E. Hayes … REVOKED.

A name struck through in black ash.

Ezra's jaw tightened.

"Your uncle tried to undo this once," he said, low. "Thought he could walk away. Burned the page. Tried to bury the book."

He looked up. His voice grew colder.

"He died choking on his own name. That's the cost of breaking it. This ain't just legacy, boy. It's weight."

He knelt, pressed the knife to Sam's shoulder, and carved the old sigil...the spiraled eye within a circle...just deep enough to scar.

Sam didn't cry out. His teeth ground together, blood running in thin lines down his back.

The earth accepted it.

The stones hummed.

And in the darkness beyond the trees, something watched.

Ezra felt it move...the presence, the hunger...brushing along the edge of the veil, just for a breath. It always came to witness.

He closed the book.

The wind died.

The moss beneath them was slick with blood and memory.

He rose. "It's done."

The elders dispersed in silence. Sam remained kneeling, shaking, staring at the steaming corpse of the chicken like he'd seen something larger than death.

Ezra turned once at the edge of the woods. "You're a Hayes now. Truly. You'll never leave this land again."

Sam said nothing.

But the cut on his shoulder burned brighter than fire.

And in the earth beneath the stones, the gate stirred...almost satisfied.

Chapter 26

Family Expectations

The Hayes land rolled on for miles, pastures stretching into the mist, fences weathered smooth by time, and fields that bore the memory of more than just crops. Tractors rusted beside barns built by hands long buried, and every stone in the farmhouse's foundation seemed to hum with the weight of history.

People in Redemption Falls didn't need directions to the Hayes farm. They just knew. It was the biggest spread for miles, a landmark etched into the local imagination, spoken of with a mix of admiration and wariness.

Sam Hayes stood like he owned the horizon, and in many ways, he did. Folks nodded when he passed, held their tongues when he spoke. He didn't ask twice for things not because he raised his voice, but because he didn't have to. Respect came easy when your family name was carved into half the deeds in the county courthouse.

But the land held more than fences and legacy.

There were stories, old ones. Whispers carried on the wind between the trees near the back of the property, where moss grew thicker and birds didn't sing. Things buried deeper than bones, older than the farmhouse itself. Traditions kept behind closed doors. Symbols carved into barn beams that didn't match any cattle brand. Ashes scattered in places no one spoke of.

Sam never spoke about those parts of the inheritance. He just honored them like his father had, and his father before that. It was expected. And in the Hayes family, expectations weren't questioned.

What had started in the green hills of the old country hadn't stayed there. It had crossed oceans, taken root in the red Tennessee clay, and grown into something darker than most folks could imagine.

And Sam... Sam tended it like he did the rest of his land...with quiet devotion.

Chapter 27

Blood and Ink

Back at Donna's kitchen table, the book lay open like a wound. Alīesung. The word itself seemed to hum faintly in the quiet, as if it were less a title than a presence. The brittle, yellowed pages curled at the edges like drying leaves, each one dense with glyphs, blocky script, and tight handwriting that writhed along the margins in spidery ink. Symbols bled across the parchment like veins under skin.

The room was dim, the overhead light flickering faintly, casting a wavering halo over the table. The air smelled of old paper and rust... something older than rust, actually, like the scent of blood dried into wood. The coffee in Donna's mug had gone cold. She didn't notice.

She sat hunched forward, elbows braced on the table's edge, eyes narrowed as she thumbed through the strange tome. Her fingertips tingled every time they passed over the pages, as if the paper held a static charge or remembered something her body had forgotten.

Across the kitchen, Beau Carter leaned against the wall, arms crossed tight over his chest. He hadn't said much since they returned, just peered over her shoulder in silence, his expression turning darker with each new page. There was a tension in him... like he was waiting for something to snap. He looked like a man standing at the edge of a cliff, listening for the wind to speak.

"This isn't just a book of old rites and sigils," Donna murmured finally, voice hoarse from disuse. "It's something else. Something more..."

Beau pushed away from the wall and stepped closer, his boots creaking softly on the hardwood floors. "It's also a ledger," he said, finishing the thought. "Yeah. A record. Blood and names and... something worse. This isn't folklore. It's an archive. A damn blueprint."

He reached out and tapped one of the margins, where a thick knot of symbols curled around a single word... HAYES.

The name had appeared again and again...always capitalized, as though it demanded reverence. Sometimes alone. Sometimes surrounded by runes and curling marks that pulsed just out of reach, like a language she almost knew.

"I've seen this kind of pattern before," Beau said, frowning. "Cults. Secret societies. Bloodline rituals. But this... this feels older. Deeper. And personal."

Donna nodded slowly, the word catching like a hook in her throat. "It is personal."

She turned the page and pointed to a line scrawled not in ink but something that looked darker... red, dried, jagged... like it had been written with a thorn dipped in something that had once pulsed in a vein.

"Alīesung"

The Singing of the Blood.

Beau's brow furrowed. "I don't think that's metaphor."

Donna didn't respond. Her fingers turned another page, and then she froze.

"Read this," she whispered, voice thin.

He leaned in, his shoulder brushing hers, the air between them tightening like a drawn string. Together, they read:

On the night of the opening, the blood of the estranged shall awaken the gate. Flesh of our flesh, taken and returned, binds the line. The mother must not stand between.

Donna's hand flew to her mouth. "I think this is about the boys," she said, her voice breaking. "Josh. Michael. My boys."

Beau was silent. His gaze drifted to the window, where the pines swayed against a gray sky, their branches whispering secrets to the wind. Then, quietly…

"You're sure Sam's their biological father?"

Her head snapped toward him; eyes sharp with offense. "Of course, I'm sure."

He nodded once; jaw clenched. "Then he thinks he's got the right. Not just in court. In blood."

Donna's fingers moved frantically now, flipping through the marked pages until she found it: a crude diagram that looked like a family tree, drawn in thick strokes. At the top was HAYES, the branches twisting downward like black roots. Near the base, faint and smudged, were two names etched in charcoal or ash:

Joshua Gareth Hayes

Michael Samuel Hayes

"No one knows their middle names," she said, barely breathing. "Not even the lawyer. Not even Sam. But this book…"

"...already has them," Beau finished, voice low and hard. "Which means he's offered them up. This is already in motion, Donna. This is a rite, and it's already begun."

A sudden knock cracked against the front door.

Donna jolted, her arm catching the coffee mug and sending it clattering across the table. It spun once before tipping, spilling its cold contents in a dark stream.

Beau was already moving, pulling his revolver from his side. He approached the door slowly, with the practiced grace of a man who'd done this before...too many times.

He opened it.

Nothing.

No one stood on the porch. Only wind. And dust curling off the drive.

Then Donna saw it.

Sitting dead center on the welcome mat was a crow's foot, shriveled and black. Red twine bound its gnarled toes together, and a bent iron nail pierced through the middle like a pin in a specimen.

Her breath caught. Her skin prickled.

Beau lowered the gun slowly and crouched beside the offering, eyes scanning every detail. "I've read about these," he muttered. "Old warnings. Territorial markers. Maybe even a claim."

Donna stood in the doorway now, staring down at it. "Then it's started. Whatever this is… it's not coming. It's here."

She turned to Beau, voice suddenly clear and steady. "We need to visit the circle that Mavis talked about. The place you said you had seen. It's described here in the book, and I think it has to do with the Sin Eaters' Circle. This could very well be the place this all comes down to."

"But first, there's someone I need to call," she said. "Someone who knows more about this kind of thing than either of us ever will."

Chapter 28

The Sin Eater's Circle

It began with the sound of wind, though the air in the room was still.

Donna had made her phone call and now they waited. Donna was still reading through Aliesung...when a strange stillness settled over everything. Her fingertips froze. Outside, the late afternoon sun filtered through the lace curtains in long, honeyed streaks. A car passed on the road. Somewhere in the house, the heater kicked on.

And then... nothing.

A pull.

Like the hush before thunder.

The room around her faded...not all at once, but in layers. Light first, then sound, then shape. She didn't feel herself fall, but suddenly she was no longer standing. No longer searching.

She was watching.

It was dusk in this place...gray and thick like smoke...and the air hummed with a kind of weight that wasn't quite grief, but close.

Trees loomed tall and bare-limbed in a wide clearing, and in the center of that clearing stood a circle of stones, blackened by age, slick with moss. Around the stones, people gathered in silence. Figures robed in wool and linen, faces shrouded in shadow, some with veils, some bare. There were no torches, no lanterns. Only fireflies blinking faintly in the underbrush and the red glow of a single ember-bed burning low at the center of the circle.

The Sin Eater's Circle.

Donna didn't know how she knew it... but she knew it.

She stood just outside the ring, unseen. Her breath caught. The air was cool and fragrant with damp earth, woodsmoke, and something coppery beneath it.

A low chant began. Soft at first... just a hum, a murmur... rising like fog from a shared memory. One of the veiled figures stepped forward, carrying a wooden tray. On it lay a loaf of dark bread, a pewter cup, and a bundle of herbs bound with red twine.

A body lay on a bier in the center, wrapped in a homespun shroud.

Donna's heart clenched.

This wasn't theater. It wasn't ceremony for show. This was old. Older than language. She could feel it in her bones. Every motion had weight. Every glance held meaning. These people weren't merely mourning the dead... they were unburdening him.

A man stepped forward from the circle, tall and sharp-shouldered, his face uncovered. His eyes were pale and unreadable, and his presence was heavy with responsibility. The Sin Eater.

He knelt beside the bier.

The chanting stopped.

The tray was passed to him with reverence, and he took it in both hands. Donna could see now...etched into the wood of the tray were symbols, some faded, some fresh, a strange mix of crosses and knots and runes she didn't recognize.

The Sin Eater placed the bread atop the shrouded chest of the dead man. Then the cup. Then the herbs.

He closed his eyes and began to speak... not loud, but clear.

"I take your hunger,

I take your sorrow,

I take the unspoken.

That which was done,

That which was not,

The lie, the wound, the wish,

I carry it now. I carry it forward.

Go in peace."

He bent forward and took a bite of the bread.

Drank from the cup.

Pressed the herbs to his lips.

The effect was immediate and harrowing. His body shuddered. His breath hitched. For a heartbeat, Donna thought he might collapse under the weight of it... but he didn't. He held. His hands gripped the tray until his knuckles whitened, his shoulders shook once, and then...stillness.

Something invisible passed from the bier to him.

And then the crowd exhaled...together...as if they had been holding the breath of the dead themselves.

Donna felt tears on her cheeks and hadn't realized she was crying.

The Sin Eater stood again, older now. Not in body, but in spirit. His face looked no different, but he bore something he had not before.

The others approached him, each in turn touching his hand or his shoulder. Offering nothing but presence. No thanks. No praise. Only acknowledgment.

And then the vision flickered...like candlelight meeting wind.

One by one, the figures began to fade, smudged by time, until only the stones remained, and the ember-bed glowed faintly, barely alive.

And Donna was back.

She staggered, bracing herself on the edge of the sideboard. Beau grasped her arms just above the elbows to steady her. Her breath came fast and shallow. Her pulse thudded in her throat.

The air still smelled of earth and ash.

"You ok?" Beau asked.

"Yeah, I... I think so."

But her heart was louder than it had been in years.

The Sin Eater's Circle was real.

And somehow, it was calling her.

Chapter 29

The Edge of the Map

The house had gone still. Too still.

Outside, the wind didn't howl...it hissed, curling around the corners of the house like a serpent searching for cracks. It dragged dry leaves along the porch in ragged spirals, scratching over the wood like claws. The gutters chattered softly, whispering in a tongue that didn't belong to weather. A storm was coming, but not the kind you could prepare for. The pressure in the air wasn't barometric...it was spiritual. The Hollowing Ground was stirring.

Inside Donna's house, the kitchen table had been transformed into a scholar's battlefield. Papers layered like fallen snow. Sigils and photocopied marginalia spilled across the surface. Ink pooled in the shallow dips of woodgrain. And at the center, like an autopsied beast, lay Alīesung...open, gutted, its pages gaping wide in fragile arcs. The parchment was dry as bone, the ink faded in places, but something about it refused to die. It pulsed faintly in the lamplight, like breath. Like waiting.

Leah Caldwell hunched over it, her fingers stained with ink and graphite, her glasses low on her nose, catching the amber gleam of the kitchen bulb. Her hair was pulled back in a frazzled knot, dark curls frizzed at the edges from hours of quiet panic. She hadn't meant to stay this long. She'd only come up from Asheville as a favor, at first, just a question from a friend.

But Donna Miller wasn't just a friend. And this wasn't just a book.

Their history ran further back than casual memory. They'd once shared late-night debates in a women's dorm lit by lava lamps and incense smoke, argued about art, journalism and Appalachian ghost lore over cheap wine and even cheaper cigarettes. Leah had been the obsessive scholar. Donna, the idealist who asked the questions professors couldn't answer. They'd drifted after college... different paths, different wounds, but something in Donna's voice when she called had pulled Leah across state lines without a second thought.

And then she saw the book.

Alīesung wasn't just a relic. It was a relic with intent. She felt it the moment she opened it, like the air changed density. Like the room tipped on its axis.

Donna now sat across from her, legal pad balanced on one knee, her pen moving in looping shorthand despite the tremble in her hand. A chipped mug of tea sat forgotten beside her, stone-cold and shadowed. Her eyes were sunken from sleepless nights, but focused. Determined. Her breath steamed faintly in the air, though the heat was on.

"I don't think this is just Celtic," Leah said, her voice hushed, reverent. She flipped a delicate page, one that crinkled like dead leaves. "There's syncretism all over it. Druidic rites, sure. But layered with Gnostic fragments, regional sigils. Appalachian root work. Binding glyphs that didn't exist in Europe."

Donna leaned closer, her breath catching. "You mean the Hayes family added to it?"

Leah nodded grimly. "Or whoever they took it from. This thing wasn't preserved. It was... adapted. The rites weren't just transplanted across the ocean. They were rewritten for the land. The soil here. The blood."

Her fingers tapped a page lined with faint black sigils, almost faded into the grain of the parchment. "These weren't in the original. These are Appalachian blood charms. Protective at first glance, but..." She traced one glyph that seemed to shift under her touch, "these are binding symbols. Sacrificial. Very old. And very literal."

Donna's throat tightened. "So, they weren't just keeping traditions alive..."

"They were weaponizing them."

Leah turned another page. In the center...three blackened fingerprints encircling a ragged hole burned clean through.

Donna's stomach turned. "That page wasn't like that before."

"No," Leah said softly. "And this..." she touched the singed edge, "this wasn't just age or accident. Someone rewrote the end of the rite."

"What do you mean?" Donna's voice came out thin.

"The original text treated sacrifice as metaphor. Dream work. Symbolic offering. But this...this revision removes the veil. Blood isn't metaphor anymore. It's the gate. And children..." Leah flipped to the final page, now annotated with frantic notes in her own hand, "they're not symbols. They're components. Part of the engine. The key to unlocking something ancient."

Leah became silent... stood and walked toward the window at the back of the kitchen facing the back yard. She stood there looking out into the darkness...arms crossed.

"You should've told me about the book sooner," she said, her voice low but cutting. "Before it got this far. We're playing catch up now."

Donna didn't look up from the counter. Her hands were wrapped around a chipped coffee mug, half full and long gone cold. She stared into it like she might read something in the surface.

"I didn't know what it was at first," Donna said. "Not what it meant."

"That's bullshit."

Donna's jaw tensed. She finally looked at her... tired, wary, but not apologizing. "You think I wanted this? That book found me just as much as I found it."

"No," Leah said. "I think you were scared. And instead of calling me... like you use to... you shut me out."

The only sound was the steady hum of the refrigerator at the end of the counter.

Donna pushed the mug aside. "You remember freshman year at App State? Lit class? You wore that jacket with the patches half hanging off and made me think you were trouble."

Leah blinked. "What does that have to do with anything?"

You sat next to me every day. Even after I blew you off that first week. You kept showing up." Donna's voice had dropped, quieter now. "You're the only one who ever did. And maybe I forgot that somewhere along the way. But I never stopped needing you, Leah."

Leah's face softened... just a bit. Her eyes flicked toward the worn ancient book... Aliesung. Its cracked leather cover looked darker in the dim light, like it had soaked up the storm brewing around them.

"You still trust me?" Leah asked.

Donna nodded once. "Yes. But I need to know you've got my back when it turns ugly."

Leah walked back across the kitchen, set her hand on the book. "Then let's turn the page."

Outside...

Beau Carter moved along the far edge of the yard, boots sinking into the soft, rain-bloated soil. The grass clung to him like fingers. The air was thick, not with fog...but with something denser. A presence. The trees stood too still, their bare limbs brittle and jagged like cracked ribs.

He paused beneath a sycamore that leaned slightly east, its roots erupting from the ground in grotesque, grasping shapes. It reminded him of old photos he'd seen of battlefield mass graves...nature reclaiming trauma.

No wind stirred the leaves.

No birds called from the branches.

The silence here wasn't peace...it was prelude.

He reached into his coat, pulled a compass from the inside pocket. Not because he needed directions, but because he needed to know what the land was saying. The needle spun wildly. Then froze. Then spun again.

North was wrong.

He stepped forward, eyes sweeping the tree line.

Then...movement.

A figure. Half-silhouetted in the gray distance, standing in the field where the old warding stones once lay. Still. Watching.

Beau squinted. "Sam?!"

The figure didn't move.

Then...without a step or sound...it began to descend. Not backwards. Not away.

Down.

As if the earth had opened its mouth and swallowed him whole.

No trace. No rustle. Not even disturbed grass.

Just... gone.

Beau's pulse roared in his ears. His hand found the grip of his revolver.

That's when he saw the trees.

Half a dozen trunks nearby bore fresh carvings...circles overlapping spirals, triangles nested inside broken teeth. The marks oozed dark sap that smelled of copper and rot.

The Hollowing Ground wasn't just stirring.

It was observing.

_____Inside Again...

Leah stiffened mid-sentence. Her fingers froze over her notes. The candle near her elbow guttered suddenly, wax spattering across the edge of the book.

"You have any wards up?" she asked sharply.

Donna blinked. "What?"

"Wards. Charms. Protective marks. Salt line. Anything?"

"No," Donna said, half rising. "I mean...I don't even know...what are?"

Leah cursed, already halfway across the room, pulling her satchel open. She tossed aside journals and folders and pulled out a small pouch filled with red string, crushed juniper, and hand-drawn sigils on paper thick as hide.

"If Sam's already begun the rites, this house is marked," she said, voice taut. "We're not preparing, we're late."

From the kitchen, the lights flickered.

Once.

Again.

Then...darkness swallowed the bulbs for a full two seconds.

And came back like a breath drawn too deep.

Then...

Three sharp knocks.

The sound echoed like hammer-strikes on bone.

Donna froze.

The front door.

She rose slowly. Leah stepped between her and the hallway...but Donna brushed past her, heart drumming like a warning.

She opened the door.

Beau stood in the glow of the porch light... his breath visible in the sudden drop of temperature. His eyes scanned past her, then locked onto Leah.

"Get your stuff," he said, voice graveled and low. "We've got company."

Behind him, somewhere in the darkness past the field, a scream rose.

Not human.

Not animal.

Something remembered.

Something hungry.

Chapter 30

The Hollowing Ground

The door shut behind Beau with a dull finality, sealing in the chill that clung to his coat and boots. Donna stood motionless, watching him, heart stuttering against her ribs.

Leah hadn't moved from the window. Her breath fogged the glass in tight, nervous bursts. She held a small bundle of what looked like twine and nettle pressed to her chest, like a prayer she hadn't finished.

"I didn't come alone," Beau said finally. "Or, I did, but something followed. I saw it." He looked down at his boots, caked in dark mud. "It was watching me the whole way through the woods. Tall. Thin. No face I could make out. Just eyes. Real still."

Donna spoke carefully. "What kind of eyes?"

Beau met hers. "Reflective. Like an animal's. But wrong. Too flat. Too human."

A silence stretched between them. Only the whisper of pages filled it, the book on the table fluttering softly despite the stillness in the air.

Leah pulled away from the window. "We can't leave. Not yet." Her voice was tight, clipped. "Not until we know what we're facing. Sam marked this spot, maybe even opened something from here. And if that's the case..."

She walked slowly to the book, one hand trailing along the table edge. Her fingers trembled, barely brushing the parchment. "We're sitting in a pressure point."

Donna sank into the nearest chair. "So, we're just supposed to wait? Let whatever's outside...in?"

"No," Leah said. "We close it. If we can."

From her satchel, she pulled out a tin box, creaking it open to reveal crumbled herbs, a coil of copper wire, three tiny vials of dark resin. She moved with slow, deliberate precision, like someone disarming a bomb.

Beau circled the room, checking windows, testing locks. When he passed the back door, he paused. "Donna."

She stood and joined him. There, etched into the wood just above the handle, was a fresh mark. A spiral within a triangle. Burned clean into the paint.

"That wasn't here before," she whispered.

Beau scraped a thumb across it. The wood hissed faintly, like it still held heat.

Leah's voice cut across the room. "That's a summoning brand. Passive, for now. It means something's already been called. We're just waiting on proximity."

Beau's jaw clenched. "Meaning what, exactly?"

"Meaning we're inside the boundary. We're part of the ritual now."

He turned away from the door. "Then we'd better start un-parting ourselves."

Leah knelt by the hearth, using the end of a broken pencil to draw a circle in the ash. "This'll hold, if nothing crosses the threshold. Nothing invited."

Outside, the wind picked up again, this time colder, sharper. Like it carried grit. The gutters rattled once, and then something struck the siding. Not hard. Just enough.

Donna stepped away from the door. "That sounded like a hand."

No one corrected her.

Leah stood, brushing soot from her jeans. "We need to ground this place. Start with iron...nails in the corners. I have some. Donna, salt the windows. Sills and seams. Beau, if you've got anything silver; a blade, coin, doesn't matter, it goes at the entrance. Ward lines won't stop a full crossing, but they might keep it at bay."

They moved as if rehearsed. Donna rummaged in the pantry for salt, three old boxes from a canning project last fall. She poured lines across each sill with shaking fingers. Beau dug into his coat, producing an old military token and wedging it into the doorframe with the butt of his revolver. Leah laid an iron railroad spike in each corner of the main room and whispered something over each one.

The book pulsed once, just a flicker of shadow across the table, like it breathed. None of them spoke.

Then…a sound from upstairs.

A slow, deliberate creak.

Floorboards.

Above them.

Donna looked up. "We didn't check the second floor."

Beau's hand dropped to his holster.

Leah shook her head. "Don't."

"Why not?"

"Because if there's something up there," she said, voice dry, "it already knows we're down here."

The wind had stopped again. No leaves. No branches. No sound but the slow groan of the ceiling above.

Leah took a breath. "The veil's rubbing thin. Sam didn't just open the gate, he anchored it. The ritual isn't just waiting, it's already feeding. Every step we take inside this structure echoes somewhere else."

Donna whispered, "Then how do we shut it?"

Leah hesitated.

"By finishing it."

Leah picked up Alīesung leading Donna and Beau to the door. Stopping for a moment to look back at them both "We have to take this fight to Sam and finish the rite!"

"Where?" Donna asked.

"The place with the circle. The place you wanted to go before. Now's the time."

With that, they headed out, enveloped in the black of night... toward the Hollowing Ground.

The Soil

Sam Hayes moved like he'd done it in another life.

Each step through the Hollowing Ground was slow, deliberate, and eerily sure…not because he understood the path ahead, but because something older than thought stirred in his marrow, pulling him forward. A rhythm. A memory he had never made.

The trees loomed taller here. Not just in height, but in presence… boughs twisted in unnatural arcs, some leaning in as though drawn by a secret they couldn't quite hear, others contorted violently, forming archways that gaped like ribs torn open. Moss hung in long, wet clumps, swaying with a breathless weight, and the bark wept sap that smelled faintly of iron and rot.

The air had teeth. Cold, damp, and unmoving, it bit at the base of his neck and slid down his spine with clammy fingers. The smell of old rain clung to the leaves, but it never reached the ground. Here, in this forgotten gully, time and weather hesitated.

Sam paused at the creek's edge. The water ran dark and glassy, quiet despite the downpour three days ago that had turned every other stream in the hills into a frothing roar. But not this one. This one whispered silence. The kind that settles deep in your ears and makes your own breath sound like betrayal.

Jutting from the muddy bank, a ring of blackened stones pressed through the soil like the tips of charred molars. Something had burned within that circle... not long ago. Not long enough. Ash clung to the edges of twisted roots, and the smell of scorched meat still lingered, faint but unmistakable.

Sam dropped to one knee, feeling the wet earth give beneath him. It was soft. Too soft. Rich with decay, full of the wet musk of rot and the copper tang of old blood. He didn't flinch as he pressed his bare palm into the center of the ring. The soil pulsed beneath his hand, once, like a heartbeat from below.

It welcomed him.

He closed his eyes and inhaled deeply, drawing in the scent of fungus, damp stone, and something else... older, feral, buried. Then, he leaned forward, and whispered words that never touched the air properly. They cracked out of his throat, rough and guttural, like stone grinding against bone. It wasn't a language he'd learned. It had taught itself to him, syllable by violent syllable, over the past year. Now it lived in the back of his throat like a parasite with purpose.

The fire pit exhaled. A thin ribbon of smoke curled upward, pale and reeking of marrow.

The sigils inked down his arms flared. First with warmth, then heat. Some were carved, the scars long since turned silver. Others painted, smeared in ochre and blood. None of them were his own. Not really. They had been given... or taken. The difference no longer mattered.

He opened a worn leather pouch, the drawstring frayed and dark with sweat and withdrew three items: a shard of bloodwood wrapped in sinew that still twitched when the moon was high, a child's milk tooth on a thread that once hung around his mother's neck, and a sliver of mirror blackened at the back with soot and something less tangible.

He placed them, one by one, into the earth. "For the tether," he murmured, voice raw. "For the key. For the gate."

The ground trembled beneath his fingers. Not a quake, not a shake… more a shiver. Like flesh remembering pain.

Behind him, the air thickened.

Not with footfall. Not with breath.

A ripple through the canopy. A compression in the pressure. A shadow that weighed more than it should.

Sam did not turn.

"You're late," he said, voice low and flat.

There was no reply, but something in the forest inhaled. Not wind, not weather… but the world itself. The trees didn't sway, yet every branch felt pulled forward, taut and listening. The weight of presence pressed against his skin like a fevered hand.

"I have what they want," he continued, gaze fixed on the blackened earth. "They'll come for it. Leah already smells the shape of it. And Donna…" A faint smile touched his lips, brittle and bitter. "She's always been good at looking in the wrong direction."

No voice responded. But something moved closer. Not with sound, but with intent.

And Sam felt it… approval, cold and massive, resonating through the marrow of his spine like a bell struck deep beneath the ocean.

His hands shook as he reached into his coat, fingers fumbling for the last piece. A length of black ribbon, old, worn smooth from handling. At its center, a crude knot, still damp. Stained dark. Wrapped in the knot…hair. Human. Still threaded with the smell of fear.

He wound it around the bloodwood and pressed the bundle into the soil.

And then, the Hollowing Ground changed.

Not with noise, but with absence.

Every chirp and rustle, every leaf-whisper and gnat-wing vanished. The forest fell into the silence of held breath. Even the air felt suspended. Stagnant. Expectant.

He stood slowly, joints stiff, heart hammering in a rhythm that no longer belonged to him. His hands twitched at his sides. The ritual was close. So close. But not complete.

One more offering.

One more tether to sever.

They called it the hollowing of the name. Not a sacrifice of body, but of identity. The cutting away of self.

He reached into his pocket and withdrew a photograph. Yellowed with age. The edges frayed. A little girl, no more than six, standing beside a stone well. Crooked braids. Mismatched shoes. A smile so wide it looked defiant.

Donna. Before the world broke her. Before she became a vessel.

He looked at it for a long time. Then let it fall.

It landed in the center of the ring, and the fire leapt... white and silent, devouring the image in less than a breath.

The trees groaned.

And from the forest's edge, something stepped into view.

It wore the shape of a man... but only barely. Flesh hung from it like garments borrowed from too many bodies. Its movements were wrong. Too fluid, too slow. Its eyes weren't eyes at all.

They were mirrors.

Sam's knees gave. He dropped hard, hands scrabbling at the dirt. A hot line of blood trickled from one nostril, and his ears rang with the high, thin whine of something just beyond hearing. His body trembled with the effort of not collapsing further.

But he didn't run.

He grinned through clenched teeth, dirt grinding into his palms. "The door's almost open," he rasped. "Let her bring the key."

The thing crouched before him. Its face stretched into a parody of empathy. Lips peeled back, too wide. And then it leaned close… not speaking with sound, but with intention.

It whispered into him.

Sam screamed.

Not out loud. Not even in his own voice.

His vision exploded… white-hot pain seared through the backs of his eyes, then turned red, then deeper, darker…

Then nothing.

Only the pulse of the earth.

Only the weight of the being.

Only the spiral, turning inward.

And Sam followed it down.

Chapter 31

Split the Earth

The Hollowing Ground knew him.

It had shaped him...cell by cell, dream by dream, until Sam Hayes no longer remembered the version of himself that had come before. That boy was dust now. Ash caught in the roots.

He walked alone.

Josh and Michael had tried to follow. Loyal, stubborn... especially Josh... but the Hollowing Ground had other plans. The barrier stopped them cold just past the ridge, where the trees thickened and the air soured. No sound reached beyond the ring of that place. They waited now, helpless, somewhere behind the black pine wall. He could almost feel Josh's fear, the heat of it like a fire smoldering behind shut teeth. Michael would be looking on, searching for a way to be brave in the face of what their father was doing.

But they wouldn't get in.

No one crossed the boundary unless the land allowed it.

And it had called for him.

Sam descended slowly, feet bare, ankles brushed by brittle stalks that hissed like old snakes. Each step was deliberate, not hesitant, but surrendered as though some ancient rhythm in the marrow of his bones knew where to place each foot before he did.

The trees leaned in, their trunks warped, their limbs gnarled into shapes that mimicked gestures… beckoning, warning, maybe even mourning. Their bark gleamed slick as flesh, soaked through with the memory of things best forgotten. Lichen clung like rot, bleeding strange pigments... ochre, crimson, the color of spoiled milk.

There was no wind here. Not even the twitch of a leaf.

The silence was a presence. Pressed close to his eardrums. Denser than fog. Holier than prayer.

Even his breath came reluctant, like it had been loaned to him by something with teeth.

Still, he felt no fear.

Not anymore.

He crossed the final ridge, and the Hollowing Ground opened before him like an incision that never healed... wide and shallow, its rim scorched with the black tattoo of fire. No birds. No insects. Just a tremor in the center, like the land was breathing from beneath.

This was where it would happen.

This was always where it would happen.

Sam stepped into the basin.

The soil accepted him. Warm, loose, wet in a way that had nothing to do with water. It closed around his feet like a mouth. The sigils inked on his skin...charcoal and blood, prayer and pain... grew hot, twitching as if they too remembered this place. Oil slicked his shoulders, sweat pooled along his ribs, but there was more than that now. Something older oozed from the symbols...a pulse in the markings, alive and muttering.

He stood in the center.

He waited.

And they came.

He heard them first. A shuffle. Three heartbeats out of sync with the land, each one thudding loud against the silence.

Donna entered first. She always would've.

Leah followed; arms wrapped tight around Alīesung like it could shield her from what she already feared. And Beau brought up the rear... jittery, hand ghosting near his holster as if steel could ward off spirit.

They crossed the invisible threshold.

And the Hollowing Ground sealed behind them, swallowing all escape.

Sam didn't speak. Not at first. Just watched.

Donna's gait was uneven. Like each step hurt. Like she was carrying something vast, unseen. Her face was thinner, her eyes bruised with sleeplessness and knowing. But there was a fire in her now, steady and smoldering. She had changed.

He admired that.

When she was close enough to see the gleam of wet ink on his chest, he finally said, softly, "Donna. I was hoping it would be you."

She didn't flinch. "You knew it would be."

He smiled. It felt like his face might crack from it. "They'll remember you, after this. You'll be the hinge the new world swings on."

But she didn't smile back. "Is that what this is to you? Legacy?"

His gut twisted. Not from guilt. From recognition.

"Correction," he murmured, voice tight.

Leah stepped forward. Her breath steamed in the chilled night air, scented with salt, iron, and something faintly floral... an old rite perfume, passed from grandmothers to daughters. She drove the iron rod into the earth with both hands.

It sang as it struck the core.

"You've twisted a rite that wasn't yours to use," she said. Her voice was low. Holy.

Sam's nostrils flared. "Twisted?" he echoed. "I inherited it. Hayes. Our name is burned into this soil. I'm just the only one who remembered."

But Donna's voice... low, clear, lethal... sliced through the air.

"No," she said. "You're the only one who couldn't let go."

That struck him deeper than any blade.

He stepped forward.

The soil groaned beneath him.

"You still don't see it," he said. "This world is skin. And the skin peels. But the bone... that's where the memory lives. The bone remembers. Blood remembers. And memory this deep? It devours. It eats your teeth from the root."

"I see it just fine," Donna said. But her hands trembled.

That's when he felt it.

Something in her...shifted.

Something in her cracked. Her posture shifted, as though her body was no longer hers alone. She staggered, trembled. The wind, what little there had been, fled in the face of what was rising from her spine. Her lips curled...her fists clenched. Her shoulders began to shake and tremble. Her teeth ground like she was trying to swallow iron and rage.

Then...stillness...she froze.

Her eyes snapped open...

...and The Hollowing Ground answered.

And she was the vessel.

Leah cried out… a word, maybe a warning.

And then it struck him. A wave. Raw power, like cold flame licking up his spine, boiling his vision. His knees buckled.

"You feel it," he gasped. There was awe in his voice now. And fear.

He had expected to take it in. To wear it like a mantle. To command it.

But she was holding it.

No… channeling it.

Tears traced clean lines down Donna's face, carving paths through ash and dust.

"You called something you couldn't control!"

"I became it," Sam snapped. A reflex. A denial.

But he already knew.

He hadn't become anything.

He had summoned it. Dressed himself in its skin. Imitated its voice.

And she...Donna...was its answer.

The one the Hollowing Ground had waited for.

The air thickened.

The rod in the soil shivered.

The wind turned inward.

Alīesung convulsed. Its pages flipped in a blur, glowing faintly, the language rewriting itself mid-flight. The ground beneath Sam twisted. His sigils burned... not with unity... but rejection.

Donna screamed.

Her body jerked and crouched to the ground. She seized. Her nails raked deep lines into the dirt. Her spine arched, mouth open in a soundless cry.

"She's burning out!" Beau shouted...stepping forward.

But Leah... eyes wide, calm as dawn... smiled.

"No... She's waking up!"

Sam staggered backward.

No. No, no, no...

"You shouldn't have come here," Sam growled.

Donna looked up. Blood on her teeth and at the corners of her mouth.

"I didn't come by choice," she said. "You brought me here!"

She stood.

The earth shivered.

"And now..." she said.

The ground buckled.

"...you'll pay the price for it."

He screamed.

Not from pain.

From rage.

The Hollowing Ground was his. It had marked him. Fed from him. He had given it everything. Memory. Blood. Years.

He was the rite.

But the rite did not care.

Alīesung ignited… no smoke, no fire, just heat and brightness and erasure. Pages curled like withered leaves. The sigils on his skin peeled away in strips, lifted by invisible hands, flaking into ash.

He felt himself unravel.

Not burn.

Not die.

Be removed.

He lunged for Donna.

She didn't flinch. Didn't lift a hand.

She didn't have to.

The light that burst from her was not divine.

It was final.

It cracked through the Hollowing Ground, split the air like thunder through bone. His body lifted. Every joint locked. Every ligament pulled taut.

The scream that tore from him wasn't human.

And then...

Silence?

No.

Worse.

Absence.

He was...

Gone.

Back beyond the boundary, Josh dropped to his knees.

Michael stared, wide-eyed, at the unmoving trees.

Something ancient had just passed through them. Not a wind. Not a shadow.

A severing.

They didn't speak.

They didn't move.

Because in their bones...

They knew.

Sam was never coming back.

Chapter 32

The Quiet Below

It took hours to carry Donna out of the Hollowing Ground.

Once the rite was completed and the Hollowing Ground closed, Josh and Michael were able to walk through… finding Beau, Leah and their mom. Their bodies moved as though they were walking through water, picking their way over roots gnarled like grasping hands and earth slick with moss and old memory. The air was heavy, thick with rot and rain that hadn't fallen. Every breath tasted of iron and ash. The forest around them held its silence too tightly, like a breath not yet released.

Donna's body sagged in their arms, limp but weighty, as though some unseen thread still tethered her to that cursed patch of earth behind them. Leah stayed beside her every step, never releasing Donna's cold hand. Her voice murmured spells too old for pages, cracked and raw at the edges. She wasn't sure they were helping. But she kept whispering them anyway, if not for Donna, then for herself.

Beau led the way, cutting the path with his boots, his revolver silent but close. His eyes scanned the dark between the trees. He didn't trust the woods. He had reason not to. The Hollowing Ground had a way of reaching past its borders. Of following.

Though the deeper violence was over, something lingered. The air shimmered faintly, like heat over asphalt, though the temperature dropped with every step. Soot clung to the trunks in thin filigrees, too precise to be natural, and the branches above twisted subtly in new directions, as if the forest had grown eyes that refused to blink.

It was Beau who said it first. "We should burn it."

Leah shook her head, tight and tired. "It wouldn't take. That kind of mark…" she glanced at the smeared ash trailing behind them "it survives flame. And if you try to burn it out…" Her gaze darkened. "You'll burn everything else too."

So, they didn't burn. They walked.

By the time Donna's house came into view, its dark windows dim behind shivering oaks, her skin was like glass left too long in the cold. Damp. Pale. Leah checked her pulse again on the porch. It fluttered, slow but stubborn, like the last beat of a drum no one wanted to play anymore.

Inside, Leah laid her on the office couch, the one with the soft dip in the middle from years of use. She wrapped Donna in two blankets and pressed a hand to her forehead. Beau moved through the house methodically, drawing every curtain, bolting every door. He settled in front of the fireplace, where the embers from the last fire still glowed faintly.

He didn't speak. Just stared into the growing flames as they caught and climbed, his shadow dancing on the walls like something trying to leave his body. Maybe he thought he could see redemption in the coals. Maybe he thought it had come and gone, and he'd missed it again.

The night passed slowly.

Leah never left Donna's side. She knelt beside the couch with a candle guttering on the floor next to her, chanting softly in the old tongue, the one that was more mountain than books. She clutched Donna's hand like it was the last branch before the fall.

Outside, the wind moved in fits and sighs. Once, something passed by the house, so quiet it might have been the breeze. But the floor groaned once, a single creak beneath weight that wasn't there. Leah's heart stilled. The presence never knocked. It didn't need to.

Donna slept through it all.

She didn't stir that night.

Nor the next morning.

She slept like the dead, but her chest rose and fell, slow and steady, like some part of her was fighting its way back from far below.

It was two full days before she moved.

No gasp. No cry. Just a breath, a slow, deliberate drawing of air, as if surfacing from something so dark and deep that light had no name there.

Her eyes opened.

For a long moment, she didn't speak. She sat up in slow increments, each motion trembling under the strain of gravity and memory. Her hands rested atop the blanket, fingers twitching faintly, like trying to remember what touch was for.

The room had changed while she slept. The air felt thicker again, like the Hollowing Ground had seeped into the walls with her. The fire snapped gently behind Beau, who hadn't moved much. Shadows clung to the corners like things unwilling to be chased out.

Leah leaned in close. "Donna?"

No answer.

Donna's gaze wandered, unfocused, walls, ceiling, floor. Like she was trying to recognize a life she had once lived but no longer owned. Her expression shifted faintly as her eyes landed on the two boys laying on the rug nearby.

Josh and Michael.

As if drawn by something unseen, they woke. Their faces lit with sudden recognition, and then they were moving, scrambling to her, arms out, tears caught in their lashes.

"Mom!" Josh breathed. "Momma!"

They collapsed into her, wrapping her in warmth and breath and the wild, terrified love that only children can give. Donna's arms came around them slowly, then with fierce urgency, pulling them in as if afraid they'd disappear.

She didn't cry. Not then.

But she held them like someone who had nearly forgotten how.

After a long moment, she looked to Leah. Her voice was rough, rasped raw from silence.

"How long?"

Leah hesitated. "Forty hours. You missed two sunrises."

Donna nodded once. That was all. But something behind her ribs seemed to let go, like a rope gone slack after holding too tight for too long.

Beau spoke from the corner, his voice low. "He's gone."

Donna turned her head slowly. Her eyes were darker than before. Or maybe just deeper...like they'd seen too far and brought some of it back.

"No," she said softly. "He's not."

Beau sat up straighter. Leah looked between them; confusion etched in the lines of her face.

Donna curled her knees to her chest, arms wrapped tight. She looked smaller now. Hollowed in a new way. Not broken, just emptied.

"He's not gone," she said again. "Just pulled back. He was too deep. Too soaked in it. That place... it didn't let go of him."

Leah's breath caught. "But the rite, you closed it. You sealed the Hollowing Ground."

Donna's eyes dropped to her knees, to hands that still shook faintly.

"I did," she whispered. "But closing one door... sometimes opens another."

The fire crackled. Outside, the wind picked up again.

And somewhere far off, in a place where roots still bleed, and stones still whisper, a door stood ajar.

Waiting. Ready.

Dawn broke gently over the ridgeline, spilling golden light through the smoky haze that still clung to the mountain side. The mist shimmered as the sun reached over the peaks, filtering through pine and oak in warm, spotted rays, hope rising quietly in the wake of sorrow.

Three days had passed since the Hollowing Ground was sealed shut and Sam Hayes had been stopped. The quiet in Redemption Falls felt different now...deeper, earned. Donna and Leah had stood on the porch that morning, wrapped in flannel and morning chill, waving goodbye as Beau Carter pulled out onto the winding road that would carry him back to Atlanta. Not to the life he'd lived before, but to something new...steadier, gentler. He had found peace here, roots where he hadn't expected them.

Leah turned and walked back inside...a satisfied grin on her face, the screen door creaking shut behind her. She paused in the kitchen, one hand still resting on the frame, then glanced back over her shoulder.

"I'd better be heading out too," she said, her voice light but edged with something softer, more careful. "Back to Asheville before it gets too late."

Donna nodded, still standing on the porch, arms folded loosely as she watched the shifting colors in the sky. The quiet between them wasn't awkward...just full, like the tail end of something that had mattered.

Leah tilted her head. "You gonna be alright?"

Donna turned toward her, that slow, grounded smile settling on her face. It wasn't the kind you put on for show. It was the kind that came from somewhere deeper, earned through fire and silence.

"Yeah," she said simply. "I'm really good."

Leah studied her for a second longer, then gave a small, approving nod.

"Alright then," she said. "Call me if ya need anything."

Donna remained on the porch taking in the morning air...crisp...clean.

Donna's phone rang, cutting through the quiet like a blade. Donna pulled the phone from her pocket then pressed the button with her thumb and pressed it to her ear.

"Hello?"

A crackle, then Dan's voice...rough, familiar, filled with an edge she hadn't heard in weeks. "Donna? Thank God. I've been trying you for days."

Her breath caught. "Dan?"

"Yeah, it's me. I'm still down in Galveston, but the storm's finally moved through. Cell towers were down, roads were flooded, power's only just come back up in some places." A pause, sharp with worry. "Are you okay?

I've been going out of my mind not hearing from you. I didn't know if something had happened. I didn't know if..."

"I'm okay," she cut in gently, voice catching. "I promise, I'm okay. I should've called sooner...I wanted to. I just... things here got complicated. There's so much I need to tell you, Dan. So much."

He let out a breath, heavy with relief. "You don't know what it's been like not knowing. Every day I was stuck here thinking the worst. I kept picturing something happening to you...or the boys."

"I know," she said quietly. "And I'm sorry. I should've found a way. I should've sent something, even just a word. But I wasn't sure what to say. Everything's been changing, Dan. Fast. And not always in ways I understand."

There was a long silence on the line, the kind that stretched not from distance, but from the weight of words left unspoken.

"You don't have to explain it all now," he finally said, softer. "But when I get home, we talk. Really talk. Can you promise me that?"

She nodded, even though he couldn't see it. "Yeah. I promise. There're things you need to know. About Redemption Falls. About... me."

Dan exhaled again; this time steadier. "My flight should leave tomorrow morning. Early. If there's no delays should be home by midday."

"I'll be here," she said, and something in her chest...tight and aching for too long...loosened just a little. "And we'll have that talk."

For the first time in a very long time, her voice didn't tremble. And for the first time in weeks, Dan's voice didn't carry worry. Only quiet relief, and something warmer underneath.

"I missed your voice," he said.

"I missed yours too."

_____ That night, no matter how many times she turned over or rearranged the covers, sleep refused to come for Donna. It hovered just out of reach, teasing her with fragments of dreams and restless thoughts. After a while, she gave up trying.

She slipped out of bed, the cool air brushing against her arms as she moved quietly through the house. Her bare feet made soft, whispering sounds against the polished wooden floor of the hallway, its surface smooth and cool like river stone beneath her soles. She rubbed one arm absentmindedly, yawning as she passed by the boys' rooms...first Josh, then Michael...each door open just enough to peek in.

Inside, the faint glow of nightlights softened the darkness. The boys were nestled beneath their blankets, small shapes breathing in slow, even rhythm. The quiet was thick, sacred, broken only by the subtle rise and fall of their tiny chests. Donna paused there, one hand resting gently on the edge of Michael's doorframe, grounding herself in the silence. Her heart eased a little, as if reassured by the pure, effortless peace of children asleep. There was nothing in this world safer than that.

She lingered a moment longer, then moved on.

In her small, book-lined office, Donna made her way to the window...the wooden frame painted white, its edges chipped slightly with time. She leaned in close, palms pressed to the sill and gazed out. The lawn outside spread like a darkened sea, freshly trimmed and gleaming faintly with dew. A row of hedges framed the perimeter, and the tall trees stood quiet, their silhouettes silvered by the soft halo of nearby streetlights. Amber light pooled around the edges of the yard, dissolving the hard lines of the world, folding the familiar landscape into something dreamlike and surreal.

Her eyes drifted across the scene...and then stopped, abruptly, pulled to a single point near the far corner of the house.

Two crows swept into view, arriving out of the night as if conjured from its very heart. They glided with together as if synchronized, their wings outstretched in measured silence. Not a beat too fast, not a sound to be heard. They wheeled in slow arcs before landing with exacting grace atop the taut electrical wire that sloped toward the gable.

Their feathers, glossy and slick, caught the light and shimmered like spilled ink beneath the glow of the streetlamp.

Donna remained perfectly still.

She stood tall, shoulders squared, and posture held with quiet resolve. Her gaze locked onto the dark shapes on the wire, unblinking...intent. The world seemed to narrow and stretch around that moment...silent, charged, unexplainable. Not menacing. Not even strange. Simply ...true.

A long breath escaped her and then a quiet smirk ghosted across her face.

It wasn't surprise that shaped her expression, nor fear.

It was recognition.

Donna just stood...

Stoic. Unshaken. Ready.